# Over Our Way

# Over our way

a collection of Caribbean short stories for young readers

edited by
Jean D'Costa and Velma Pollard

Orders: please contact Bookpoint Ltd, 130 Park Drive, Milton Park, Abingdon, Oxon
OX14 4SE. Telephone: (44) 01235 827720. Fax: (44) 01235 400454.
Email: education@bookpoint.co.uk.

Lines are open from 9 a.m. to 5 p.m., Monday to Saturday, with a 24-hour message
answering service. You can also order through our website: www.hoddereducation.com

First published 1980
Second edition 1994

First published by Pearson Education Limited
Published from 2015 by Hodder Education,
An Hachette UK Company
Carmelite House
50 Victoria Embankment
London EC4Y 0DZ
www.hoddereducation.com

20 19
IMP 10 9 8

Set in 12/13½ Baskerville
Printed in United Kingdom

ISBN 978-0-582-22580-0

# Contents

# Acknowledgements

We are grateful to the following for permission to reproduce copyright material:
the author, Mark D. Alleyne for his short story 'Amy and I' first appeared in Short Story Contest 1977 run by BBC Caribbean Magazine, produced by BBC Overseas Regional Services; BIM and the author, John Wickham for his short story 'Casuarina Row' appeared in *BIM* Vol 14, No 56; BIM and the Saunders Estate for the short story 'The Statehood sacrifice' by the late, Dr. Ronald Saunders, appeared in *BIM* Vol 13, No 51; BIM and the author, Ralph Prince for his short story 'The waterwoman and her lover' appeared in *BIM* Vol 13, No 53; the author, Jean D'Costa for her short stories 'The bicycle' and 'Devils of Rose Hall'; Andre Deutsch for the short story 'Peeta of the deep sea' by Michael Anthony in *Cricket in the Road*; the author, Merle Hodge for her short stories 'Millicent' and 'Jeffie Lemmington and me'; the author, David E. King for his short story 'The paddy-man'; the author, Millis Nicholls for her short story 'Heart man' which first appeared in Short Story Contest 1977 run by BBC Caribbean Magazine, produced by BBC Overseas Regional Services; the author, Velma Pollard for her short story 'My mother' which

first appeared in *Jamaica Journal* Vol 9, No 4, 1975; the author, Olive Senior for her short story 'Ascot' which first appeared in *Jamaica Journal* Vol 8, No 4, 1974; the author, Judy S. Stone for her short story 'The owl and the poodledog'; the author, Calvin Watson for his short story 'The legend of Talon'.

# Over our way

## A word to the reader by Jean D'Costa

Over our way lies a world of flame trees and hot beaches rimmed with hills, of raucous laughter in the market and shouts in the street, of bare feet running down dusty lanes and across burnt savannahs, splashing beside the boats of fishermen or inching up the ringed bark of coconut trees. Our way stretches far, so far – all the way to Detroit and Birmingham and Toronto, and all the way through time to Dahomey, India, Scotland and China. Our way splits like a spider-road leading all over the face of the earth.

Our voices echo down our way, throwing out words from Yoruba and English, Hindi and Gaelic, French and Arawak, and singing the music of a dozen languages living and dead. Listen to the voices from over our way and you will hear the whisper of people moving through time and space across oceans and continents in ships and aeroplanes, on foot and on mule-back. Our way reaches from the grandson programming a computer in Minneapolis to the son on a Venezuelan oilfield to the mother selling cloth in Port of Spain to the grandmother making bread in Castries, and still further on and back to the great-grandfather distilling rum in Port-au-Prince and the great-great-grandfather, a negro sailor buried in Marseilles. It is a long way.

A long way, full of laughing, weeping, blessing, cursing, explaining, quarrelling, accusing and lamenting.

We cannot see the beginnings or ends of our way, but we can tell some of the stories of what happens over our way: stories which we alone can tell, stories about our friendships, our lonelinesses, our games, our crimes, our sorrows and joys, our triumphs and dreams.

The stories in this book are a handful gathered from over our way: there are thousands more, waiting for you to tell them.

Jean D'Costa
St. Andrew
Jamaica

# Millicent

## Merle Hodge

For Faith Ann Gore and Nona Magdalene Mitchell

Fourth Standard was a very ordinary class. They came to school for nine o'clock like any other class – or most of them cane to school for nine o'clock – for when the bell rang, Clem and Harry were usually just pelting across the savannah. Clem had to tie out his grandmother's goat before he came to school and Harry had to deliver bottles of milk. They were neighbours, and nearly every morning they dashed into the school-yard together and managed to slide in at the back of the line just as Mr Greenidge was closing the gate. Anybody who arrived after the gate was shut had to stand outside and wait until Mr Greenidge was ready to let them in and lead them to the Headmaster's office.

Fourth Standard was very ordinary. They had as many fights as anybody else. They fought over the duster because everybody wanted to clean the blackboard; they fought over who was to be at the head of the line in the mornings; they fought in Miss Aggie's parlour at recess-time and at lunch-time, fought and pushed like anybody else to get their dinner-mints or sweet-biscuits or tamarind-balls. And they didn't fight when it was their turn to clean the latrines; then, they just ran and hid all over the place.

There were twenty-two girls and eighteen boys, so the girls always won when the class played cricket or tug-of-war, girls against boys.

Fourth Standard had its Duncey-Head and its Bright-Spark like any other class. Joel Price couldn't read further than page nine. He was stuck at page nine for so long that he could say it by heart with his eyes closed, but when Miss turned the page and he saw page ten he would hang his head and his eyes filled up with water. And Emily Joseph was so bright that everybody said that her mother gave her bulb porridge in the morning and bulb soup in the night.

Miss was nice sometimes. She didn't beat as much as Mr Gomes or Mrs Davies, and she didn't beat for silly little things like forgetting your pen at home or getting all your sums wrong.

But she got very angry if somebody talked while she was talking. Sandra and Shira were always getting into trouble, because they chatted and chatted like a pair of parrots all day long. Miss promised them that when we went on the zoo outing she was going to put them in the big cage with the parrots and leave them there. Miss said the parrots at the zoo had a nice big roomy cage big enough for two talkative young ladies to take up residence, and the parrots would be glad of their company.

Other things she would beat for were not doing your homework, and stealing. When something was stolen, nobody knew how she found out who the thief was, but Miss was always right. As soon as she learned that there had been a theft, she tapped the ruler on the table to call the class to attention. Then she stood and stared at us; she looked at our faces one by one, very slowly, and when she had looked at everybody in turn, she started again from the front row, while everybody sat and held their breath; and then her eyes stopped at one face and everybody breathed again, and all turned to see who the culprit was. In Fourth Standard you couldn't get away with stealing.

Miss was nice because she took her class outside more often than anybody else. The other children all envied Fourth Standard because whenever the afternoon got really hot we would be seen filing out towards the savannah. Anybody who talked or made any noise on the way out would be sent back to sit with his book in the empty classroom, but of course nobody was willing to run this risk, so we filed out silently and in the most orderly manner.

Miss said that Fourth Standard was the worst class in the school, but we knew that she'd said the same thing to every Fourth Standard class she'd had, so we didn't believe her. For, all things considered, Fourth Standard was no better or no worse than any other class; they were a very ordinary class.

And then Millicent came. Millicent came and brought pure ruction.

One Monday morning there she was, sitting in the third row in a bright red organdy dress and red ribbons and smelling of baby powder. She was sharing a desk with Parbatee and Eric and Vena and Harry. The desk was only made for four, but Miss put her there because Parbatee and Eric and Vena and Harry were all very small and didn't quite fill up the bench. But there was Millicent sitting in the middle, with her elbows sprawled on the desk on either side of her, and her skirt spread out on the bench, so that Parbatee and Eric were squeezed together at one end of the bench, and Vena and Harry looked as though they were about to fall off the other end. Millicent sat like a queen in the middle.

The other four sat cramped for the whole morning, barely able to write, but not daring to complain, for Millicent and her red organdy dress filled them with awe.

But by mid-afternoon Millicent had taken over so much of the bench that Harry really fell off his end. All we heard was a little crash, because Harry was not very big (in fact, we called him 'Mosquito'). We heard a crash and a small shriek and Harry was sitting in the aisle ready to burst with anger.

Everybody laughed, the class was in uproar. Miss was laughing helplessly too, but then she made her face stern again and tapped the ruler on the table. Harry picked himself up and stayed standing in the aisle, looking at Millicent in such a way that if looks could kill, Millicent would have dropped down dead in her red organdy dress.

'Millicent, you will sit at the end,' said Miss.

'NOPE!' said Millicent and she folded her arms, pouted her mouth and stayed where she was.

Everybody was shocked. This girl must be crazy! We stopped all our laughter and stared in amazement. Even Harry forgot to be angry and stared dumbfounded at Millicent, then at Miss, from one to the other.

There was complete silence. We were a little excited, waiting to see what would happen next, looking at Miss's face.

'Come out here, ma'am,' said Miss.

Millicent still sat with her arms tightly folded and her mouth pushed far out like a pig-snout. Then Miss started to get up, her chair grated on the floor. Our hearts beat faster. This crazy girl didn't know our Miss – she wasn't afraid of her in her organdy dress, she would put the ruler on her, organdy dress or no organdy dress.

But when Millicent saw that Miss was going to come for her, she suddenly sprang up and pushed Vena off the bench to get out. Vena didn't fall right down, but she hit her elbow on the edge of the desk, and that made her so angry that she flew at Millicent and landed her a cuff right in the middle of her chest. Miss rushed down the aisle and parted them.

15

Millicent was crying loudly, saying she was going to tell her Auntie June, and she didn't like this old dirty country-school, and her father was going to come and take her back to Belmont . . .

Miss clapped her hands sharply:

'Get your spelling books, everybody outside, no noise; and you ma'am, if you make one more sound, you will sit down right here by yourself.'

The rest of us were nearly outside already, Millicent stood sniffling still, rather bewildered at the sight of the classroom emptying around her. Then she wiped her nose and followed.

Out on the savannah we quickly settled down, some sitting on the grass, some on the old tree trunk. Joel brought the chair for Miss.

Millicent stood apart and looked on scornfully. We soon forgot about her, because there was a nice breeze blowing, and Miss asked us easy words – even Joel was able to spell two whole words, so he was wearing a broad smile. Everybody forgot about Millicent. We didn't even know she had walked off.

And then suddenly the ground seemed to shake and we heard something like thunder mixed with screaming, and we looked and saw this red shape flying across the savannah towards us. In one second there was a stampede. We had tumbled off the tree trunk, those on the grass had scrambled to their feet, spelling books were lying scattered on the ground and the whole of Fourth Standard was running, pelting towards

the school, everybody screaming with all their might.

Mr Jeremy's bull was loose! And nobody knew how Millicent had managed to offend Mr Jeremy's bull, but it was chasing her furiously, pounding after her, snorting and cursing her in cow language, and she was tearing across the grass, her red organdy dress flying in the breeze.

Nobody looked back until we were inside the schoolyard. Then we looked out and saw Miss bringing Millicent, who was crying bitterly, holding one of her ribbons in her hand, the sashes of her dress hanging down.

The next morning Millicent appeared in a bright yellow organdy dress and yellow ribbons. She sat at the end but placed her big plaid bag on the bench beside her because, she said, she didn't want either Picky-Head Congo Vena, or Roti-Coolie Harry near her. Vena went and complained to Miss.

Again we held our breaths. Once, when we had just come up to Fourth Standard, she shared licks for half an hour one afternoon when she got the news that at lunch-time a little fight between Carl and Deo had grown into a war with nearly the whole of Fourth Standard divided into two gangs calling each other Coolie and Nigger. She told us that everybody's great-grandfather was both a Coolie and a Nigger – Deodath's great-grandfather was a Nigger and Carl's great-grandfather was a Coolie, because

Coolie and Nigger just meant beast of burden, and that all our great-grandparents were made to be, but if that was what we wanted to be then she would lick us like beasts of burden; she sent a boy to borrow Mr Gomes's strap, went on the rampage and shared out some unforgettable licks. That was the last of that.

When Vena went and complained to Miss, she shot up and strode down the aisle to Millicent.

'Pick up your bag, ma'am,' she said.

Millicent held on to her bag and Miss yanked her out of the seat and marched her to the back of the class. She told the children in one of the back rows to take their desk to the front, while she sent some others to get one of the old desks from downstairs.

This ruction lasted for about fifteen minutes and we enjoyed it thoroughly. At the end of it all, the back row children were installed in front, and in the back row, in an old rickety desk for four, sat Millicent and her plaid bag. Millicent in her yellow organdy dress. She was not very pleased.

At recess-time she picked up her bag and walked solemnly to Miss Aggie's parlour (everybody else *ran* to be there first). When she got there, she didn't join the pushing and jostling; she just stood, looking so angelic in her yellow organdy dress and yellow ribbons that Miss Aggie was impressed, stopped serving us and called out to her:

'What you want, little girl?'

Millicent smiled sweetly, took one step forward and the whole unruly crowd of us fell silent and automatically parted in two, making way for her. She walked to the counter and put down a dollar bill. A whole dollar bill! Our eyes nearly fell out of our heads, and a low sound of 'Oooooo!' rose from the crowd.

'Ten cents' dinner-mints please, and ten cents' paradise plums, and six cents' saltprunes, and . . .' Miss Aggie moved from bottle to bottle, her eyes widening all the time.

Millicent spent the whole dollar. She stuffed all that she had bought into the bag and turned to go. We were following her every movement. She walked out of the parlour without looking right or left.

By afternoon recess Millicent sat on a bench in the yard surrounded by a court of seven. These were the Chosen Few: Clem, Diane, Shira, Joel, Anthony, Fazeeda and Gayle. Their mouths were full, and as they chewed away, their eyes were fixed admiringly upon Millicent.

The next morning Millicent arrived in a pink dress, and Miss asked her when she was going to get her uniform. She said her Auntie June hadn't got it yet.

At recess-time as she sat holding court, she was heard to say loudly to her group of admirers:

'She think I don't have my uniform hanging up in my press? What I must wear uniform for? I not wearing any uniform. I have a whole press full of clothes and shoes and toys . . .'

The news reached Miss, and that afternoon Millicent went home with a letter from Miss to her Auntie June. The next morning Millicent came to school wearing a blue overall, white blouse and a scowl on her face. She was very sour indeed.

That morning Clem came to school without Harry. Millicent had told him to have nothing to do with Harry or she wouldn't talk to him any more.

At lunch-time, we started up a game of cricket. Faraz and Anthony were the best batters, and Gayle could bowl down wickets like peas, so everybody wanted them on their side. Somebody went to look for Gayle and Anthony. They were in the parlour with Millicent and they didn't feel like playing cricket. So the rest of us played a stupid, dull game.

When Sandra came back from lunch she went in search of Shira, for she had so much to tell her, and they hadn't had a chance to talk in class all morning, because Miss had kept her eye on the two of them. She didn't get to talk to Shira at morning recess either, because she spent the whole of recess in the latrine. Her mother had given them salts the day before, and that was one of the things she had to tell Shira about – how her mother and her grandmother had to run after the six of them, round and round the house, until they caught them one by one and held their noses and made them drink the salts. She was dying to get into a cosy conversation with Shira.

She looked around the savannah for her and didn't find her. Then she went into the school-yard, walked around, and spotted her on the tank with some others playing jacks. She ran happily towards her, calling out her name:

'Shira! Shira!'

Shira turned around to see who it was and then coldly turned her back. Sandra thought she hadn't seen her and went right up to the tank and touched Shira on her shoulder.

Shira brushed her off: 'Leave me in peace, nuh!'

Sandra was flabbergasted and didn't move. Millicent drew herself up.

'You wash your foot before you come in the dance? Shoo! We don't want any picky-head tar-babies here.' And the rest of the gang giggled.

Sandra ran away and hid in a corner until the bell rang.

By the end of the week Millicent's gang had grown to fifteen. They stopped playing on the savannah. Millicent brought a fancy skipping-rope, jacks, ludo, dominoes and pretty story-books. With these, as well as all the sweets she bought, she held them captive at recess and at lunch-time.

She got them to run to the parlour for her, do

her homework, fetch water for her in her pretty Mickey-Mouse cup.

The rest of us didn't know what to do. Nobody any longer thought of going and telling Miss on her. For there were a lot of us who would have given anything to join Millicent's gang and didn't want to offend her. And even those who hated her were afraid of her.

Fourth Standard became a sour, quarrelsome class. Millicent's gang didn't have much to do with the rest of us, and the rest of us had more fights among ourselves than ever before. We began to call each other 'Cassava Nigger' and 'Pelorie Coolie', terms we had learnt from Millicent. Almost every time we started a game it ended in a fight. Somebody always said the scorekeeper was cheating or the bowler was aiming the ball at the batsman's belly for spite.

And Millicent reigned supreme. She managed not to get any licks because her homework was always done, and she couldn't get into trouble for talking in class when there was nobody sitting with her.

And she didn't get any licks at home either. Everybody knew that her Auntie June let her stay up until any hour she wanted, even midnight; that she never had to wash dishes or sweep; that when she got home from school, she just sprawled off in an armchair and her Auntie June took off her shoes and socks for her and immediately brought her ice-cream and cake; that her mother, who was in America, sent her a box full of clothes and shoes and toys every week ... Millicent was a heroine out of a story-book.

We no longer considered her to be sitting in disgrace at the back of the class in the desk all by herself. She was a princess sitting on a throne, and nobody was really good enough to sit on the same bench as Millicent.

Of course Miss knew that all was not well in the class. She called Harry and asked him why he and Clem didn't come to school together any more. Harry's eyes filled up with water and he wouldn't say a word. She called Clem and asked him. Clem wriggled uncomfortably and said his grandmother made him get up earlier to go and tie out the goat, and he couldn't wait for Harry again. Tears started to run down Harry's cheeks. Everybody felt ashamed, but nobody would say a word, for Millicent was sitting surveying us all from her throne at the back of the class.

Miss sent Harry and Clem back to their seats.

'So nobody in this class has anything to tell me this week,' she said, 'not even the news-carriers. Hm.'

We sat and squirmed. Miss looked at everybody then she looked straight over our heads to the back of the class and said, slowly and terribly:

'Pride goeth before a fall.'

Nobody had the faintest idea what this meant, but we knew it meant something very grim and unpleasant. Everybody knew that she had looked at Millicent as she said it, but no one dared even glance back at Millicent. Nobody would risk offending Millicent.

Matters grew worse over the next few weeks. Millicent threw Joel out of her gang. She had sent him to the parlour with ten cents to buy three cents' dinner-mints, five tamarind balls and a packet of chewing gum, and he came back with twenty dinner-mints. She told him he was so stupid he had no right to live. Joel cried for two days.

We all knew that Millicent would now be looking around for a new member to replace Joel, so we were extra courteous to her for the next few days. We remarked to each other how nice Millicent's hair-style was, how clean her crepesoles, how enviable her complexion; we vowed within her hearing that we couldn't stand blackie Picky-Head Niggers and greasy Roti-Coolies. We declared that we found Miss to be an out-of-place frowsy old hog, always trying to boss people about. We smiled nervously at Millicent, who ignored us completely.

And soon Millicent's verdict was made known: the new member was Christine Reece. The rest of us were heartbroken. We now hated Christine Reece with all our might, but continued to do everything we could to get into Millicent's good books.

Nobody bothered to start any games on the savannah any more. We hung about the schoolyard and sulked, casting envious sidelong glances at Millicent and her gang. And Millicent continued to look upon us with scorn.

Then it was the end-of-term test. Millicent announced that she was coming first, that Emily Joseph didn't know as much as she knew because she didn't have all the books that she had, and Emily's mother couldn't buy Brain Food for her like *her* mother sent from America.

And there was no question in anybody's mind – of course Millicent was going to come first. She was the prettiest, richest, luckiest, bravest, quickest, funniest, cleanest, healthiest child in the class, so naturally she was also the brightest; she didn't even have to say so, for everybody knew. Even Emily Joseph knew. Emily Joseph wouldn't dare come higher than Millicent.

Miss gave the arithmetic test first. Millicent finished long before everybody else and closed her copybook, while Emily Joseph was still writing and counting on her fingers. When we came out, Millicent boasted to her gang that she had got out all the sums in two twos.

In the afternoon we had dictation. Millicent wrote rapidly, never stopping to look at Miss.

The end-of-term test lasted for two days, and the next day at lunch-time Millicent gave a 'party' for her gang to celebrate her success in the exam. She had brought apples from home, and pretty paper cups with Mickey Mouse on them. She sent messengers to Miss Aggie's parlour to buy soft drinks and sweet biscuits. They had a feast, and we hung a little distance away pretending not to notice them; but if Millicent had thrown an apple stem to us, we would have fought over it like dogs.

The bell rang and we went in. Millicent's gang were rubbing their bellies and making sounds of satisfaction, and Millicent sailed in with her head in the air.

When we had settled down, Miss said, 'Test results', and everybody shouted 'Raaaaaay!', including Joel, who was never anywhere but last.

'Where to begin?' Miss asked. 'Top or bottom?'

There was commotion for a while, some shouting 'Top! Top!', some shouting 'Bottom! Bottom!', and some even shouting 'Middle!'

Then we realised that Millicent's gang was shouting 'Top! Top!', so everybody shouted with them. Of course if Miss started from the bottom of the list, Millicent would have to wait for forty-one names before she heard hers, which was, of course, at the top.

'Okay, okay, I'll start from the top. Quiet, or I won't read them at all.'

She picked up the list, put on her glasses, and everybody looked at Millicent with admiration and then turned to look at Miss again.

'First – Emily Joseph.'

We jumped. Emily looked frightened. Nobody dared look back at Millicent. Miss was reading on. Fifth, sixth, seventh . . . We were worried. She must have forgotten Millicent. Eleventh, twelfth, thirteenth . . . Decidedly something was wrong.

By the time Miss had got to thirtieth we were paralysed. Nobody could move. We held our breath. Thirty-second, thirty-third . . . You could have heard a pin drop. We wanted to stop Miss, to make her start over again, because she had skipped over Millicent's name.

'Thirty-ninth – Faraz Mohammed. Fortieth – Joel Price. Forty-first – Millicent Hernandez.'

Several seconds passed before we could breathe again.

Then we heard a giggle, and we couldn't believe it had come from our class. But it had, Vena had her hand over her mouth and was shaking with laughter. She looked at Harry. A smile spread over Harry's face. He put his head down on the desk and giggled. Snickers came from different parts of the class. Miss was calmly putting away her list.

The giggles and snickers grew. Soon the whole class was laughing as loudly as we had laughed the day Harry fell off the bench. Miss turned her back and cleaned the blackboard.

When she had finished cleaning the blackboard, she gave us the ball and sent us outside, because, she said, we were the most unruly class in the whole school, and in the whole of Trinidad and Tobago.

We poured out onto the savannah.

'Football!' somebody shouted.

'Girls against boys!' said another.

'Not fair!' said a boy's voice. 'It's twenty-three girls against eighteen boys.'

'Which twenty-three?' asked somebody. 'It's only twenty-two girls. Let's go!'

It was the best football game we had ever had. Nobody won because there was so much laughing and rolling about that we forgot to keep the score. The goalpost kept falling down and Joel wet his pants.

Somebody shouted: 'Mr Jeremy's bull!' and we scattered, screaming, in all directions; and when we realised there was no bull, we lay down on the grass and laughed till we were weak.

Then we tried to start the game again, but Clem grabbed the ball and ran off with it, and everybody ran after him, so he threw it to another boy, and soon the game turned into Sway, and when it was Sway, the boys always managed to keep the ball, the girls never got hold of it . . .

And it was only twenty-two girls, because Millicent was sitting in the school-yard, all by herself.

# The bicycle

## Jean D'Costa

For Joyce Johnson

It was Ma's fault in a way.

'You children should see your Uncle Rupert riding his bicycle in Kingston!' She would stop whatever she was doing and hold out her hands as if she had got hold of the handlebars of the bicycle. 'When the buses and the cars go swisssh! past him, you just see him make a little move one side, quick-quick, like fish runnin' from Brother Shark! Swisssh-swisssh! And the bike just slides through the crowd easy as cheese!'

Uncle Rupert and Ma were twins. That was why they boasted about each other and always knew if something was amiss with the other.

'Can't I have a bicycle, *please*, Pa?' begged Ernest.

He was better at begging than any of the others. The others were Hazel, Marion, Christine and Donnie, who was only two and didn't count. Ernest was the Boy of the Family, as Grampa put it.

And then Grampa was as bad as Ma.

'Rosa, how you expect the Boy to be on time for school? He has to go all that way with no bus or pick-up to get a ride. And then he must go to Scout meetings and cricket practice.'

Ernest was twelve and in his last year at primary school. The girls were all older and going to secondary school. Of course Donnie was too small to go any further than Grampa's chair under the mango tree in the back yard, where the two of them got up to all sorts of mischief.

Pa had the only cool head in the house except for Hazel, who was the eldest and resembled her father down to the last inch of her wiry frame. All the others took after the Dawes side and looked like Ma.

And that is why the whole thing was so remarkable.

Ma had been a very pretty girl in her time, but inclined to fat. Uncle Rupert was the only postman in the whole city of Kingston who weighed two hundred pounds and rode a bicycle. If you saw him you would feel sorry for the bicycle. And of course Ernest was coming up the same way.

When you looked at Ernest Keane, leaning against the school fence and picking his teeth during break-time, you wouldn't expect much from that round ball. But nobody ever called Ernest anything but Ernest to his face or behind his back. The last boy who made the mistake of calling out something about 'Fatty-from-the-circus' is now going to another school. In the cricket team they call him Jumbo Jet, and that's because he is the best all-rounder, batsman,

31

bowler and wicket-keeper, in the four schools around Woodside in St. Mary. And it isn't fat. It's muscle. I know.

Pa kept saying 'Yes, but . . .' about the bicycle; parents have to say that sometimes. Pa had a steady business as a butcher, but it could not pay for everything *and* stretch to a bicycle for Ernest.

Then Grampa stepped in. I mean he really took a step.

'ERNEST!!!!' he bawled. 'Come down to the square with me.'

That was quite normal; Grampa took his evening constitutional every day with the Boy of the Family. Pa said 'The two Boys of the Family', because Grampa was the person who taught Ernest all the most useful things about Life – like making sling-shots, whistling, fast and slow bowling, the meanings of those words which decent people NEVER use, most of his arithmetic, and how to make model ships and houses. Grampa is Pa's father, and he used to be a tailor before he came to live at Woodside. Pa complains that Grampa never told him half the things which he tells Ernest.

Well, that afternoon they went off as usual, and Grampa stopped to chat with old Mrs Walker, his good friend and adviser from years back, while Ernest picked six yellow-heart breadfruit off the big tree round the back for her and ate three slices of cake. He was almost as fond of Mrs Walker as Grampa was. Then they went on down to Teacher Gordon, and that was where they heard about the raffle.

One of the prizes was a bicycle, and the tickets cost fifty cents, or five shillings as it was in those days. Between them Grampa and Ernest had thirty-five cents.

Grampa borrowed a sheet of paper from Teacher Gordon and wrote a note to Pa, which he sent off by Ernest. Pa had shut up the shop and gone out with Zacky the handyman to look at a pig for Saturday's market, so Grampa scratched his beard and borrowed the fifteen cents and another sheet of paper from Teacher Gordon and wrote him an IOU in a splendid copperplate hand, signing it with a flourish.

'See there, boy! That's how men deal business with each other!' stated Grampa. He then took nearly two hours to choose the ticket, an arduous task made easier by the consumption of three bottles of beer while Ernest had nearly a gallon of lemonade. In the end Grampa chose a number which was the sum of his age and Ernest's plus seven, a serious number. It was ticket no. 99, and anyone in Woodside can tell you that *that* is a good number in a raffle.

'They're giving lots of different prizes,' Teacher Gordon began to explain. 'You could win a camera, or a cricket set with bat, ball, pads and so on – that's very good! And they have other things your daughter-in-law would like: bedspreads and a tea-trolley and crockery . . .'

Grampa cut him short:

'We're going for the bicycle. They can keep everything else. Come around on the weekend after the draw and watch Ernest riding it.'

The drawing of the raffle was set for six weeks' time, and you heard nothing in the house from Grampa and Ernest but bicycle, bicycle, bicycle until Ma and the girls were sick of hearing the two of them carrying on.

'Mind you don't set your heart too much on that raffle and let it kill you,' said Ma as a joke. It was only a joke. No one could have known.

But on the morning of the draw Grampa was up very early, got all dressed up and went walking round the backyard very impatient and all ready to go. All he had for breakfast was two cups of strong coffee.

To tell the truth, everyone was excited. Somehow that bicycle was going to be Ernest's before the day was over.

The drawing of the raffle was to be held at the end of the school concert that afternoon, and as most of the children were in the concert they soon went off and were to be seen no more that day. Ma had all her Saturday work cut out for her; Pa went off very early to the shop, and it was only Donnie who was left with Grampa.

Pa and Ma feel very bad about it, but the doctor says nobody could have done anything about it.

Just as Ma was finishing tidying the kitchen,

something made her decide to take a glass of orange juice for Grampa. And that was when she found him slumped in his chair under the mango tree, with Donnie still playing quietly beside him. He had had a stroke.

For the rest of that day, nobody was much interested in the concert or the raffle. The doctor came, and as Grampa had regained consciousness, he let him stay at home. But Nurse Phillips came to spend the night.

And nobody took much notice when Teacher Gordon came himself to ask after Grampa, bringing with him the glittering new bicycle.

Oh, yes, they had won. And that is perhaps the last time that Ernest cried as a child. He took the bicycle silently and put it away in the shed round the back, and that was where, alone in the dark, the tears ran down his cheeks unnoticed.

Pa made him learn to ride.

'You mustn't disappoint your grandfather. He's getting better, and when he can come outside again, the best thing you can do for him is to show him how well you're doing!'

And Grampa did get better slowly, but there were some queer things. He couldn't remember anything about the bicycle or the raffle, and his right hand and leg trembled all the time. But slowly, slowly, he got better until he was able to sit up in his room, and then walk about the room, then sit on the verandah and finally walk to the gate and back. But he still forgot things and Ma had to be on her guard that he didn't go out alone. Sometimes he thought he was back in his old house at Lime Tree Garden, and wondered why the furniture was strange. Sometimes he asked for his sewing machine and worried about finishing orders in time for Christmas.

All this while he never saw the bicycle, because Ma thought it might get him too excited while he was still far from well.

And so in a way she blames herself still.

It was coming near to Easter when that hot, dry wind blows and even St Mary is short of rain. Grampa went off by himself one day and was found over at the Church looking for Rev. Hastings. Teacher Gordon brought him home and told Ma he shouldn't be wandering around like that, he might come to some harm. Rev. Hastings had christened Pa and was dead these twenty years.

The very next day Grampa ran away from home.

Ernest was the first to get home from school and as he turned the corner near the house he knew something was wrong. He suddenly found himself running instead of walking, and as he got near the gate he could hear Ma sobbing and crying out.

'Grampa's gone! Grampa's gone!' was all she could say.

Ernest took one look at her and ran back to the gate. The next-door neighbour had seen nothing.

He ran on. Down the hill there is a bus stop near to Mrs Franklin's gate and *she* can tell you who got on and off the bus at that stop for the last forty years.

'Yes, I saw the old man take the bus, but I didn't think anything funny about it. And is the last bus for Kingston too. Where you say he's going?'

But Ernest was back up the road like a shot. He almost had to shake Ma.

'Grampa's gone to Kingston!' he shouted.

Ma sobbed louder and did not hear the rest of what Ernest was saying.

'Kingston! All that way by himself!' Her sobs doubled.

A cold fear gripped Ernest but he did not stop to argue. Ma thought that he had gone off to find Pa, so it was not until Hazel came home and went back to fetch Pa and Ernest that they discovered that Ernest was missing too. Then Pa said,

'He's gone on the bicycle.'

And the bicycle was no longer in the shed.

It is nearly eight miles from Woodside to Troja, the nearest town on the bus route to Kingston. The road goes up and down, up and down, on its way there. A bicycle would go much more slowly on the hills. And after Troja, village follows village along the main road down to Bog Walk with its general stores, factories and of course the highway to Kingston. Ernest's mouth grew dry and cold as he thought of all of the places on that long road down through Troja, Harewood and

37

Riversdale. Grampa had an old friend in Troja: he might stop there. Or he might stop in Bog Walk nine miles further on. He was well known in Bog Walk in his younger days. He pushed these thoughts to the back of his mind and rode on.

Ernest asked at every bus stop if anyone had seen Grampa; he was terrified that he might have got off the bus and wandered away.

And now the road was paved, but still the bus was ahead of him, gaining all the time, he thought. It was late evening, almost night, when he got to Knollis, just outside Bog Walk. He had been lucky, for the last few miles were downhill and he had picked up speed. He was lucky enough to meet two women who had just got off the bus at Knollis. The sweat ran down him like a river and his chest hurt.

'Yes, that nice old gentleman? He sang for us and told stories all the way. He says he's going to Bog Walk on business, some tailoring work he has to see to, and also to pick up his grandson's bicycle.'

Ernest rode off fast.

Nobody knows to this day how he did it. While Pa was searching in vain for a car or van to take him after the bus, Ernest had covered that last mile between Knollis and Bog Walk in time to catch the bus even before it left, and to find an empty gravel truck bound for the North Coast and willing to stop in Richmond, or maybe even go a little further out of the way.

At ten o'clock that night, everyone except Pa was sitting on the front porch, talking in whispers and holding their breath sometimes. Even Donnie was up, and not chattering or yelling for once. Ma had stopped crying, but she just sat there and didn't say a word all evening. The girls were scared.

Just then, bright headlights shone down the road and a huge truck pulled up at the gate, its horn blowing loudly.

'Saviour, my Lord, what is this now?' cried Ma, clutching the arms of her chair. 'Don't tell me he's dead and they're bringing home the body!'

Loud singing burst on their ears.

'John Brown's body lies a-mouldering in the grave!'

Grampa's baritone and the truck-driver's bass went well together, the effect somewhat spoiled by Ernest's alto which kept changing to treble on the high notes.

Out they tumbled from the truck, lifting the dusty bicycle carefully down.

'BUT HIS SOUL GOES MARCHING OOOOOOON!'

# Casuarina Row

## John Wickham

Elizabeth Godding was a mild-eyed little girl who lived among a swarm of sisters and two brothers, Courcey and James, down in the village near the market. She was as demure and as shy as a nun, but she had a ferocity of imagination and such a startling idiosyncrasy of speech that, although by the village will and testament she was my girl even before we were twelve, I was never able to guess from one moment to the unpredictable next what random arrangement of words would issue from her mouth. Nor was I ever able to imagine what went on behind the bland brow, what images paraded before those lambent eyes that in the middle of a sentence would go all vacant and far away.

Every Saturday morning Elizabeth came running up Breakneck Hill. She dashed around the side of the house past the fowl run, climbed over the railings of the front verandah and, panting as if she had just manoeuvred her escape from the darkest of dungeons, still demure, presented herself to Grandfather, who sat in his rocking chair contemplating the sea and expecting her.

Grandfather greeted her exactly as he greeted adults, seriously and solemnly, his manner bearing no trace of condescension, but rather the faintest glow of delight that he should be the object of her faithful regard.

'Good morning, Elizabeth,' Grandfather said every Saturday morning, as if it has been years and not only a week ago that he had greeted her.

'Good morning, Elizabeth,' Grandfather said, taking from his pocket the silver-wrapped, cream-filled chocolate that was his Sabbath blessing.

'Good morning, Grandfather. Thanks.' Elizabeth would cup her two hands together to receive the blessing whose bounty would threaten to overflow the space offered by a child's two hands. And then she would curtsey, and, if I were not around, ask Grandfather for me.

'George,' Grandfather would shout, 'Elizabeth is here.'

And so Saturday would begin.

Grandfather had planted at the edge of the garden a line of casuarinas which were about three or four years younger than I was and about as high off the ground. Our Saturday, Elizabeth's and mine, would begin with a visit to the casuarinas. Immediately after she had eaten her chocolate, as if it were magic food, Elizabeth became Mrs Gullett and I by the consent of my affection for her, Mr Gullett. The Gulletts were Elizabeth's figments, the creatures of the same unfettered imagination which had made of the row of casuarinas a collection of families each of which possessed its own singular distinct and inviolate identity.

Mr and Mrs Gullett we were, an elderly couple rendered childless by the fact that our children were 'away' – a clever Elizabethan contrivance which permitted the receipt of countless letters from them, and thus the exercise of a tireless imagination: snow twenty feet on the ground, and fog so thick that you could cut it with a knife, and tall buildings, and clothes never seen, and accents and languages never heard in our prospect corner of the world. Letters came from all corners of the world containing reports of every variety of adventure; train journeys, monuments, accidents, calamities, all products of Elizabeth's (Mrs Gullett's) vivid imagination.

Slowly the Gulletts, arm in arm and as genteel as adults, made their way from tree to tree, from house to house, family to family, to whom my Saturday wife Elizabeth had given the most original of names.

'Good morning, Mrs Bucket,' she greeted the slender, tired-looking casuarina at the head of the row, at the same time nudging me into a proper good morning. She was always apologising to a casuarina for my lack of manners or my absent-mindedness, saying that I had her in barracks.

'He doesn't mean anything by it,' she said, 'but you know what husbands give.'

And I would find myself murmuring an apology to a tree and asking after the health of

Mr Bucket and the five little Buckets standing
sedately in a row at their mother's right hand. Mr
Bucket was a fisherman and was never to be found
at home; if he was not out in the boat, he was
in the rum shop, Elizabeth said that Mrs Bucket
said. But he was a kind and thoughtful friend and
was always making us presents of fish; there was
hardly a Saturday morning Elizabeth did not leave
the Buckets without a bright blue chub or a red
snapper or a handful of flying fish in her basket.
But Elizabeth thought Mrs Bucket dull and said
that she was a numb drum. The first time I heard
her say the words I thought that Elizabeth had lost
her way again in the treacherous overgrowth of
her amazing vocabulary, and I said that surely she
meant 'humdrum'. Elizabeth gave me such a look
of pity that there and then I realised that a numb
drum was really what she meant Mrs Bucket to
be – a particularly unexciting instrument of the
orchestra. Elizabeth said that Mrs Bucket was a
complainer, and I had to take her word for it.
Certainly more than once while they chatted and
Elizabeth asked how the children were getting on,
I heard a thin wail issue from Mrs Bucket which
sounded almost like the whine of the wind in a
casuarina. Elizabeth never let Mrs Bucket talk too
much; she herself always had to give the news of
our own children: George was on an expedition
in Arabia, and Lysander, the second boy, was
winning *olé* after *olé* in the bullrings in Madrid.
We had a daughter named Cleopatra, who was

studying to be a doctor and was so busy that she didn't have time to write very much, but she was well when last we heard from her. Elizabeth said that she didn't much like visiting the Buckets, but since they lived at the head of the road she couldn't very well pass the house without saying hello.

'They would feel bad,' Elizabeth said, 'and it wouldn't look good.' And I agreed with her that we should not snub them, especially when we could put pot on fire in the certainty of a fish or two every Saturday morning. I believe that Elizabeth thought there was something mischievous in my argument, for that was one of the times when she accused me of being opposite.

The Buckets' neighbour was Sophie the Grand-duchess. That was the only name we, or rather, I, knew her by. Elizabeth probably knew more about her than she told me, for they were always whispering together and giggling like little girls. There was no Grandduke in evidence and Elizabeth and I, naturally, were too discreet to ask. Sophie had a little daughter who, Elizabeth said, was a Marchioness, but I never saw her. She was sickly and Elizabeth was for ever advising Sophie about cures, one of which was so startling that, even accustomed as I ought to have been to Elizabeth's fantasies, I could not help protesting.

'You must bathe the child in black molasses,' Elizabeth said, 'that's the best thing for what the child has.'

'Black molasses!' I began to argue.

'Yes, black, b-l-a-c-k, black molasses,' Elizabeth said firmly so that there should be no doubt. And I shut up. I was always finding out that I knew nothing at all about the most ordinary things.

Sophie the Grandduchess, who always carried on her conversations with her arms akimbo, did not very much credit the efficacy of Elizabeth's prescription and bluntly refused to try it on the grounds that it sounded to her like obeah, a piece of recalcitrance which nearly broke the friendship. When, on the following Saturday morning, Elizabeth asked after the Marchioness and was told that she was better, she thought proudly that the recovery was the result of a bath in black molasses three times a day, and was furious (that is, as furious as Elizabeth could get) when Sophie told her that she hadn't tried the recommended cure. Sophie, arms at hips and swaying slightly (Elizabeth swore that she could smell the rum on her breath) must have made some kind of offensive or sarcastic remark about native cures or bush medicine which, to tell the truth, escaped me. But the next thing I knew was that Elizabeth grabbed me angrily and, muttering something about people being ungrateful, you did your best for them and they didn't evaluate it, led me away from the house.

For a few Saturday mornings after that incident we used to walk past Sophie's house without even a good morning, Elizabeth holding her head high in the air and I a little sheepish and ashamed of her unexpectedly rude manners.

Yet, all in all, Sophie was good fun and Elizabeth, when they were on speaking terms, used to spend what seemed like hours every Saturday morning chatting and laughing and carrying on while a little way off and out of earshot I fretted in silence. Elizabeth said that she liked Sophie because she was uphazard, which I had the wit to understand was the very opposite of numb drum. From where I stood I could barely hear Elizabeth's whispered gabble as she exchanged the latest with Sophie. I used to think at first that Sophie did not do much talking, but when Elizabeth began to tell me the things she said and how lively she was, I had to change my opinion. Once, Elizabeth said, Sophie draped herself in potato-vine leaves and danced a mazouk in the moonlight to the great delight of all the neighbours. Elizabeth's opinion was that as Sophie was a noblewoman she didn't have to care what anyone thought of her. Up till then I had thought that noblewomen used to care a lot what people thought of them, but I came to learn later that Elizabeth was, as usual, right.

One Saturday morning as we left the Buckets, I saw Elizabeth dab her eyes with her handkerchief and noticed that she gave no sign that she was stopping to see Sophie. I was fairly sure that they weren't going through one of their things, for I hadn't heard Elizabeth say anything about *that*

Sophie. I was more than curious to know what had happened. Elizabeth kept looking furtively at the house as if she did not see Sophie standing there, arms akimbo as usual, and I wondered what I ought to have known.

'We are not stopping to say hello to Sophie?' I asked.

Elizabeth burst into tears. I asked her what was wrong, but I could not understand what she was saying between the sobs. After a while she stopped crying and said that she thought I had known that the little Marchioness had died and that Sophie had gone away.

Sophie's house did not stay empty for long, not for more than two Saturdays. One morning as we passed what I thought was the empty house, I said that I wondered how long the house would remain shut up, and Elizabeth asked me if I hadn't heard that someone was moving in the following week. I began to tell her that the only person who gave me news of the people in Casuarina Row was herself, but she didn't seem to understand what I was saying and I let it go. I asked her who was moving in, and she told me the story of Nick the Kick.

Nick, Elizabeth said, had lived in Panama for years and years and had a lot of money, but he was very mean. He had a reputation as a woman-beater and lived alone, doing his own washing and cooking and cleaning, which Elizabeth said, showed that he was not a noble man. All this news

Elizabeth picked up from the neighbours, for she refused to speak to Nick, who would be standing at his front door or sitting on the verandah when we did our Saturday morning round. Elizabeth said he had no manners and ought to speak to us first as he was the stranger. But Nick, who was a rough sort of person, did not observe these niceties. I tried to tell Elizabeth that the kind of person I guessed Nick to be wasn't likely to care very much whether she spoke to him or not. After three or four Saturday mornings I began to feel silly passing Nick's house with him standing in full view, picking his teeth or whistling or just standing and staring at us while we pretended that he didn't exist. So, one morning I raised my arm and said, 'Hello, Nick.' And immediately Elizabeth said, 'Hello, Nick,' and stopped.

If you had heard Elizabeth, you would not have believed that she had ever said what she had about Nick the Kick. She didn't give the man a chance to speak. It was all, 'I was going to stop in, but I was letting you settle first. There's always so much to do when you move house. We moved house once and it was two years, two years before we settled. Not so, George?'

And as I nodded in support, all I could think was, 'Cool, Elizabeth, very cool!'

Nick must have fallen for Elizabeth's interest, because she went on talking to him, asking him about Panama and telling him that her eldest brother Courcey once had a friend there and that she herself had always wanted to see Panama and did he see where they made the hats? And Nick, whose tongue was said to be so foul that it wanted scrubbing with pot soda and carbolic soap, that same Nick who had no respect for women – Nick the Kick was silent. Elizabeth overwhelmed him, clearly.

'And how do you like these latitudes?' she asked Nick.

I wondered if Nick understood what she meant and whether he was as confused as I was when she first used that word to me. But I said nothing, remembering that Elizabeth used to tell her friends that I was simple. I expect Nick understood, because I didn't hear him ask her what she meant. Elizabeth went on talking about the neighbours, telling Nick about the Buckets next door and about Sophie and her daughter and all the households along the road: the Outs and their swarm of children (Mr Out was a baker and Elizabeth said that the children were always covered in flour from head to toe); and the Yellow Lady, whom Elizabeth refused to call by her proper name and who lived by herself and, Elizabeth whispered, was a witch because she was in the habit of talking to herself; and in the last house, right at the very end of the road, Miss Providence, who was a Seventh-day Adventist and whom we never saw since she was always at church when we passed by on Saturday mornings, but who always left us, wrapped in brown paper on her doorstep, a loaf of coconut bread she had made before sunset on Friday.

I grew impatient while Elizabeth recited all the gabble-gossip of Casuarina Row into Nick the Kick's unexpectedly receptive ears.

'Come on, now,' I said.

Elizabeth said goodbye to Nick and I heard her promise him that she would call around the next day.

When we moved off I said, 'But tomorrow is Sunday, Elizabeth.'

At first all she said was, 'You're jealous,' and I was thinking about that when she said, 'Yes, I know tomorrow is Sunday, but I'm Mrs Gullett on Sundays too.'

I thought her voice had an edge to it, but I couldn't let go. 'We never go out visiting on Sunday, you know that very well, Elizabeth Gullett,' I said. My world was upside-down and I could not understand what had happened or was happening.

'But we can, if we want to, and if you don't want to, George Gullett, I can go by myself.' She sounded as if she were more than play-play angry, and I made the thing worse by asking, 'Do you like Nick the Kick?'

'Don't be stupendous,' she said, but I didn't understand whether she meant I was stupendous to ask or whether the likelihood of her liking Nick the Kick was so remote that the question was an absurdity. Whichever way it was, I reckoned that something had happened to put an end to the Gulletts' Saturday morning calls.

'It is stupendous to believe that casuarinas are people,' I said.

Neither Elizabeth, Godding or Gullett, made any comment. But one of them, I don't know which, hooked her right arm in the crook of my left elbow with a sedate and proper gesture of affection and I remembered that my right arm, the sword arm, had to be left free to draw in defence of my lady.

But it was Elizabeth Godding who, suddenly turning the full glory of her quiet grey eyes upon me, asked me, not at all in the tone of possession which was the one she used whenever or wherever I was involved, it was that Elizabeth who asked me, as if for once my answer to her question would be of some importance, 'George, do you love me?'

I told my Grandfather about this and even he, wise as he was, was unable to fathom the depths of so innocent yet so terrible a question.

Nothing in my thirteen or fourteen years had prepared me for the profundities of this confrontation, for I recognised, foolish and uxorious as I was, that this was more than a question to which I could answer yea or nay, as Elizabeth would say. So I hesitated. I thought that the seriousness of the question deserved more than an impulsive answer. I thought: Nick the Kick, adolescence; whatever Elizabeth, Godding or

Gullett, it didn't matter which, may have guessed me to be, I was not a complete fool. Why did she want to know? I said to myself, 'Now, George, however you answer this question, you will be in the wrong. Think, think.' And I thought of all the Saturday mornings, the visits, the uneasy nonsenses, the play-play realities and, after all the thinking, I said, 'Yes, Elizabeth, I believe I love you.'

'Why did you have to stay so long to answer?' Elizabeth asked, and strutted off clutching her basket with the blue chub and the bonito Mrs Bucket had given us that morning.

Saturday morning came again and Grandfather sat in his rocking-chair. It was long past ten o'clock and no Elizabeth had put in an appearance.

'No Elizabeth this morning, George?' he asked. 'I wonder what's wrong.'

And I, who had no secrets from Grandfather, did not wish to and did not know how to say, that the casuarinas he had planted were, jump high, jump low, only a row of trees.

# The Statehood sacrifice

## Ronnie Saunders

Latona looked out upon the sun-baked earth where a few chickens scratched desperately to grub out a meal from the barren nothingness. They reminded her of her Mamma, always struggling, always scrounging, always slaving to put something in their bellies and on their backs, while her father, with inebriated ecstasy, buoyed up his spirits and drowned the canker that nagged at his conscience.

Latona shuddered. She looked down at her helpless baby brother, curled up around a strip of cloth, a hint of a smile lingering on his lips. With eight mouths to feed, Mamma hadn't wanted another. Besides Mamma was getting old and she, being the eldest, had to do all the housework and still go to school.

The little girl gazed at her baby brother again. She couldn't help reaching for his cheek. His smile softened. Latona buried her head in his tattered clothes, tears filling her eyes.

She straightened up, thoughtfully fingering the dainty pink ring she had fashioned for herself. No, Mamma hadn't needed another child, born to feel life's raw uncompromising bitterness; to struggle, at first with a fierce urgency in the mire of despondency; then to wallow aimlessly; and then to sink down, haggard and spent, like her Mamma. Dave would be better off elsewhere. Not that she didn't want him close to her, but how could you love him and keep him here? Yet, his brothers and sisters had endured it all. Hadn't they survived? Yes, until now. And what could they show for it? The swollen guts of malnutrition, sores and toe-boe, and hungry faces.

Yes, Dave would be better-off elsewhere.

At school, she had heard that poor families often gave their children away. Mrs Lynton, one of her school teachers, took care of that sort of thing. She would tell her about Dave on Monday.

No!

She couldn't let him out of her life so soon.

Suddenly, Latona remembered about Statehood. Mrs Lynton had said that its coming meant that everyone must help his brother by doing great sacrifices. Only then would everybody be truly happy, and St Vincent, her home, would be a better place in which to live. Everyone in her class had to make a Statehood sacrifice – not just stop buying rarie-tarie or tullum, but something really meaningful. Latona had thought about it, but it just didn't make sense.

Every day living was a great, big sacrifice. It wasn't her fault for thinking that Statehood meant that the 'state' would put a hood over every Vincentian's head to shield him, not only from the wind and rain and sun, but from the hunger and poverty and disease that made life a wretched, miserable, endless nightmare.

Latona went to see Mrs Lynton. At first she was a little sceptical, but gradually, Latona convinced her.

'Yo' see, Miss, is nine ah ar-we, an' Mamma always sick an' so is I does ha' fo tek care ah dem. Is ah good boy, Miss, an' 'e want somebody nice to look aftah 'e.'

'What about your family?' Mrs Lynton asked.

'Fam'ly? We nah got none, Miss. Only Mamma an' Pappa.'

'What's his name?'

'David, Miss.'

'All right, Latona, we'll try to help David.' She stood up to go. Latona clutched her hand.

'Miss ...' she faltered. 'Miss, try get a good Mamma fo' 'e. Yo' heah Miss?' Latona searched her face. 'Yo' heah, Miss?'

Mrs Lynton nodded.

'Miss Smart would be a good mother,' she thought. She was always saying how badly she wanted a child. She was well-off too. Her little shop on the corner was doing fine. Mrs Lynton decided to ask her.

On Thursday, she told Miss Smart about the boy.

'How old is he?' she asked.

'Three. Pretty poor family too! Nine children. And the mother's old as anything.'

'The father drinks a lot, I hear.'

'You know them?'

'Douglas used to . . .' Douglas was Miss Smart's brother.

'The girl's a good child. Used to help me clean up sometimes. God, Molly, the old lady can't take on another kid. You know it too!'

'Don't like those country folk too much, you know, Clara. No manners . . . no training . . . rude . . .'

'Not the Smalls, Molly. You forget Thomas, the eldest boy?'

'I remember him. Douglas used to buy salitire for him everyday. You don't get those nowadays. Pity you had to drink so much to get them down. Tom and Dougie murdered my limes.'

Both women laughed.

Mrs Lynton got up, 'Okay, Molly,' she said, 'see what you can do. They really can't afford it.'

'I'll think about it later and see them.'

Late on Saturday evening, Miss Smart arrived. Latona went inside, a strange, lonely feeling pervading her whole body.

'Mamma! Mamma!' she said quietly. 'Miss Smart come.'

Latona's mother sighed wearily and straightened her clothes. Latona met Miss Smart outside.

'Evenin', Miss Smart, Mamma inside,' she said, fidgeting with the clothes the Salvation Army had given her.

'Thank you,' Miss Smart smiled.

At the doorway, she stopped. The room was extremely small, and dark. A feeble candle flickering in a corner served to accentuate rather than brighten the foreboding gloom. Inside everything in the room seemed feeble – the tottering furniture, the crumbling walls, the decrepit old woman sitting at the table.

It was a bizarre picture, smelling of decay, seething with discord, stooping to defilement.

Outside, it was a sweltering eighty-five degrees. Listless. The leaves barely stirred. The heat was unbearable, but Miss Smart felt cold – cold and alone.

Latona's mother rose. 'Evenin', Miss Smart.' Her voice was barely audible and just as feeble.

Miss Smart saw a frail, gentle woman, prematurely aged with a look of mild complacency offset by the hint of sadness in her eyes – an indelible sadness etched out by years of forced toil and worry and pain. Miss Smart saw a woman flirting with death, needing it, yet shunning it.

Latona's mother saw a woman with a pleasant face, a woman who had already seen something of what life was all about. She had that indefinable air of motherhood about her. Happy, and fairly well-off; she was what David ought to get. Latona's mother saw a woman of tenderness and love, a mother for her son.

Miss Smart sat down. 'Where's David?' she asked.

Latona brought him in.

'He's three, isn't he?' She didn't wait for a reply. 'Did he sleep today?'

'Not much . . .'

'What about food? Does he get a fair amount every day? Milk?'

Miss Smart kept up the questions, all the while regarding the boy with a critical eye.

Suddenly Latona burst out, 'Oh, Mamma, please nah leh 'e go now. No! Mamma, no!' Latona buried her face in her mother's lap, her tiny body trembling with each sob, her voice pleading with all urgency and hope. 'Nah now, Mamma. Wait till tomorrow . . . Tomorrow, Mamma. Please, Mamma, please.'

The old woman and Miss Smart looked at each other sadly.

Miss Smart walked over to the child. 'Come, Latona,' she said, 'you mustn't cry like that. After all, David would be happier with me. Don't you want him to be happy?'

Latona turned around and looked at Miss Smart, her eyes ablaze. 'Ah love him. An' ah want him to be happy . . .'

'Then you must make a big sacrifice, Latona.'

Latona got up quietly and went inside.

With Miss Smart, it wasn't easy either. Discussing at garden parties the spiralling birthrate, then saying pathetically, 'If only I could adopt one of our poor helpless babies . . .' was far easier than doing this, because deep inside she didn't want *this*. She wanted a foreign child, from America or

61

England perhaps; someone to show off at these same garden parties, no one remembering your 'fervent' desire to adopt a Vincentian child.

It has happened to all of us at some time, and Miss Smart was no exception. We despise our own. Because he is born in poverty? Because he is one of us? And none of these any fault of his. Knowing our miserable own with subtle contempt, we have yearned for the foreigner.

But Miss Smart had made her decision. The English could well take care of their own. But St Vincent, on the threshold of Statehood, must solve her own problems, must accept her own, not only because it was right, but because the success of any new state relies utterly on the pride and dignity and love that can come only from her people.

Inside, Latona spoke softly to her brother. 'Yeh, Dave,' she said, 'new Mamma gwine tek care o' you, see, an' yo' mus'n gee no trouble ah'tarl. Yo' mus' be good, yo' heah? An' when you get big, you mus' come see we. Heh, tek dis to 'member me.' Carefully, Latona removed her pink ring and put it on his finger. 'Doan' loss it, yo' know.'

She rubbed his cheek with hers.

From outside, her mother said, 'Latona, bring out de chile.'

The celebrations were over. Latona returned to school, where Mrs Lynton asked about everyone's Statehood sacrifice. When it was Latona's turn, she stood slowly, borne up by such grace and

pride that everybody turned to stare at her. The room was hushed. The little girl looked frail and forlorn. She raised her eyes and met Mrs Lynton's gaze. Her lips quivered as she tried to speak, but nothing came. Latona lowered her head again, looking down at her bare finger, unable to keep back the tears that flooded her eyes.

# Amy and I

## Mark Alleyne

Looking back from when I was eight I couldn't remember once not living without Amy next door. She and I were always friends, except for a few disagreements here and there which we ironed out between ourselves. And the bond that linked Amy and me also linked our parents, because my mother and Amy's were good friends (or so I thought).

During the vacation Amy and I played together. Sometimes she came over to our yard and other times I went over by her. Amy had a ball, and we usually played 'bat an' ball' in the yard.

Amy could bat well and sometimes she struck the ball way over the fence and I would have to look for it. Not much to say for two eight-year-old girls, does it? But we loved 'bat an' ball' and very seldom we reluctantly changed it for something else – like skip or hopscotch.

Once during the vacation when our mothers were at work, Amy and I were playing in the yard. Amy was batting. I tossed the ball up to Amy hoping she would strike it up into the air and I might catch it. But Amy did otherwise and flung the bat around, and before I got my eyes on

the ball again, bits of glass were scattered about the ground. Amy had broken one of the panes out of the kitchen louvre-window.

Amy dropped the bat and came down to me.

'See what you do now?' she stated with wide eyes.

'I ain' do nothing,' I retorted. 'You is the one who hit the ball.'

'You is who bowl it. If you didn't bowl it that way I wouldn't have hit it so.'

'You lie!' I shouted.

Amy held down her head and I sensed that she wanted to cry.

'Jen, you goin' tell 'pon me?'

'No,' I said. We never betrayed each other in a case like this. 'Come, Amy, let's clean it up and then decide what to do.'

I went to get the broom from the corner of the yard.

Amy followed. 'You goin' tell?' she asked again.

'No,' I assured. 'Come, let's clean up quick.'

After we had gathered up the bits of glass in a paper bag, Amy threw it over into the canes behind the fence.

'What we going do with that now?' I asked her, pointing across to the louvre-window, beginning to feel the tension rise within me. Amy was crying: a long stream of tears ran down the sides of her contorted face. Feebly she dropped down on the cemented floor of the yard and sat there crying, wiping her eyes lightly with her fingers.

'I ain't goin' tell,' I said again gently, sitting down beside her. She rested her head upon my chest and abruptly she stopped sobbing and we got up from the ground.

'Now you keep quiet about it an' I will keep quiet about it too, see?' I said.

Amy nodded in agreement with me.

All the fun was gone and it was odd thinking how a few minutes before bat an' ball was so much fun till all that happened. Amy and I walked across the yard to the kitchen door and when we got there I wiped her eyes with the hem of my dress.

'You sure you ain' goin' tell 'pon me? 'Cause I would get licks.'

I nodded.

'I goin' in, 'cause I ain' feel so good,' Amy said, and slowly she went through the kitchen door and closed it behind her.

When our parents came home, everything seemed to be going fine until late in the evening when Amy's mother came knocking on our door.

I had lain in bed the whole afternoon waiting desperately for forthcoming events.

When Mummy heard Amy's mother knocking, she went and opened the door. I bounded out of bed and, with a racing heart, went into the dining-room where they were.

'Jen tell you that they break one o' my louvres today?' Amy's mother asked my mother.

'No,' my mother replied, and she turned to me. 'Jen, you all break one of Maggie's windows today?'

I shook my head, concealed fear mounting within. 'I ain't went out there for the whole day. I was in bed reading,' I lied.

'An' look Amy say that you went out there,' Amy's mother said, trying to trap me.

'Yeah, I went out there but we only play a game o' cards, that's all.'

'You sure?' Mummy said.

'Yes, please,' I replied.

'Amy say that she went to sleep and when she wake up, she find the window break up,' Amy's mother said. 'I feel that Amy know who the person is but she trying to protect them, 'cause I know that if Amy did do it, she would've confess.'

'You trying to say that Jen do it and Amy trying to protect she?' my mother said, beginning to get hot.

'All I saying is . . .'

'Jen say that she ain't do it, an' she ain't do it. Whatever Jen say I believe!' my mother cut in firmly.

'Wha' if Amy say that she ain't do it an' I believe she too?' Amy's mother retorted.

'Wha' foolishness you coming in here talking?' my mother went on. 'Jen ain't break your window!'

And so the quarrel went on. They went outside into the road and most of the people from the neighbourhood gathered and formed a ring around them. There wasn't any bodily contact; they clapped their hands and pranced around each other like excited turkeys, each swearing that her child hadn't broken the window . . . . (Grown-ups are so stupid.)

I was peeping at them through the window and when my mother came in, she took down the strap and in a frenzy of anger, she gave me the flogging of my life. From next door I heard Amy screaming and knew that it was the same on Amy's side too.

The next day our parents went to work. I stayed inside; but I listened for Amy to call all the same.

After a while Amy came and called: 'Jen . . . Jen.' She was at the back door.

I went and opened the door.

'Come. Let's play skip,' she said, taking my hand.

'Let's play outside,' And when she saw that I moved with naïve reluctance, she went on, 'Mummy won't know.'

I smiled at ease. 'Yes, let's play skip,' I said.

# Peeta of the deep sea

## Michael Anthony

Peeta panicked. There was nothing he could do. He was trapped. Trapped with hundreds of others. The Monster had come and was slowly, surely, dragging them from the deep. Peeta swam through the excited crowd to try the bottom. Then he tried the top again. The great Monster had encircled them completely. There were millions of holes in its great hands, but none large enough. If only these holes were a little larger. Peeta tried to push himself through one of the holes again. He squeezed and squeezed. Great tails lashed around him. Not only he but the whole crowd was in desperation. He tried to ease himself through. The threads pressed against his eyes. If only his head could get through. He pushed again, hard, and the pain quivered through his body. Down to his tail. He turned around. But it was no use trying it from that end. His tail was much wider than his head. There was nothing he could do. He heard the breakers roaring above now. That meant they were nearing the shore. Peeta whipped his tail in fury. The Monster was closing its hands gradually. He could feel the crowd pushed against each other. He was knocked about by the giant tails. Good thing

71

he was so small and could avoid being crushed.
Around him were his friends and his dreaded
enemies. The bonito was there, the killer shark
was there. None of them thought of him now.
They were all trying to escape.

The killer shark, he thought again. The Monster was taking the killer shark too. Shark, bonito,
herring, cavali – they were all the same to him. A
giant swordfish charged the threads desperately.
The shark turned on its belly in vain to swallow
the Monster. Instead it swallowed a jelly-fish.
There were cries now above the surface. Below,
the Monster grated on the sand. The shore! They
had reached the shore! Frantically Peeta flung
himself against one of the tiny holes. He gave a
cry as the scales tore from his back – then a cry
of joy. He was free! Free!

He lunged forward below the surface. He could
feel the weight of the breakers pushing down on
him. He could hear the terrible roar which from
the deep had sounded like a whisper of music.
He looked back a little. There was only a tiny
streak of blood behind him. He would be all
right. He would be all right. Down, he went.
Farther away and down. Faster, faster he swam.
His tail whipped the white foam, pushing him
forwards like a spear. Down he sped, rejoicing
in his tinyness; if he had been a little bigger,
he would have been dying on the shore now:
the fateful shore. There had been those who
had actually come back from that world. This

was one of the greatest mysteries. It was hard to believe that any fish had come back from the shore. But some said they had been there, and had talked of that awesome place of no water and no fish. It was hard to believe this. But so had it been to believe about the Monster. But the Monster was real enough now. His mother had always warned him. He looked back a little. There was no more blood now. Down, down he swam. Deeper, farther. Deep, deep, until the sound of the breakers was only a bitter memory, and the sea was not sandy but blue and clear, and until far, far away in the distance, green with the fern and the tender moss he saw the rocks of home.

A thrill ran through him. He squirted through the water as if a new verve had possessed his body. His tail whipped the white and frothy foam. 'Mother!' he thought, 'Mother!' And he dived headlong towards the green rock.

'Mother, I am home,' he gurgled.

The mother stared at him between the rocks. She noticed the bruised back. She was cross, yet the fact that he had returned made her feel thankful inside.

'Peeta!' she exclaimed.

'I am home,' he said.

'Wherever have you been to? Whatever happened?'

She was sure he had gone playing among the rocks and had lost his way. And that he had

74

bruised his back swimming carelessly or romping with the shingles. Peeta was like that. He always went far away to play. He always ran away to meet the corals and the anemones and his other friends of the deep sea.

'Where have you been?' she said.

'Mother . . .' Peeta hesitated. 'Mother . . . the Monster . . .'

The mother went cold with shock. Her eyes gleamed white and there was fear and horror in them.

'Peeta, I warned you, I warned you. You wouldn't hear. Why did you go near the surface?'

'Mother . . .'

'Keep away from the surface, I always tell you. Keep away from the shore!'

'Mother, the Monster is everywhere.'

'He can't come between the rocks. He never comes here.'

'Mother, I can't stay all day between the rocks. I have friends everywhere. This morning I promised the corals – '

'This morning you promised nothing!' gulped the mother. 'You nearly promised your life. Keep here between the rocks. Play with the moss and the fern. Here you are safe.'

'The Monster isn't always here,' said Peeta. 'Sometimes I swim out to my friends. We see wonderful things. Sometimes we go up to the surface to see the sun. It is dark here below. Up there it is bright and very strange. When I grow up, I will go often to see the sun, and to hear the music of the waves, and to watch the winds play on the roof of the sea.'

'Hush up,' the mother gulped. 'It is more beautiful here between the rocks. It is more beautiful here because it is safe. Tell me, how did you escape? It is very odd. No one escapes from the Monster.'

'Oh,' said Peeta, and he told her. He told her how he was just playing and how very suddenly he found himself against the great hands of the Monster. He told her how terrified he had been and how he swam to the bottom to escape, but he could not. And even at the top he could not. For the hands were everywhere. The hands with the million tiny holes. He told her how there were hundreds of others caught like him, even the killer shark. She gulped, and shrank back, and he said yes, the killer shark. And he told her how the great hands had closed gradually around them and pushed them all together, and how they were all frightened and desperate, even the killer shark. He told her how the breakers had pounded over them and how they were dragged on the sands of the shore and how he had actually heard the voices of the shore. Then he told her how he had flung himself desperately against one of the holes, while the threads cut him and the pain shot through him, but how he had discovered himself free at last in the wide ocean. And he laughed as he said this part, for he remembered himself speeding through the water, faster than anything.

But the mother did not laugh. In fact she was gloomier than before. For Peeta was a wayward fish. She knew she could not change him. She knew that with all her advice she wouldn't prevail upon him to keep away from the open deep, and from the surface, and from the sound of the breakers near the shore. She knew, too, as well as he, that it was his tinyness that had saved him. But he was growing fast. In the next few months he would be no baby any more. She shuddered to think what would happen then if he made such a mistake again. Certainly that would be the end. Yet, as he grew, he would become quicker. The carite was perhaps the fastest fish in the sea. But as far as she had heard, the hands of the Monster were deep and wide and stretched far beyond the bounds of speed. Therefore she turned away sadly and swam to a dark corner of the rock to meditate.

The fully-grown carite was, indeed, the fastest fish in the sea. Peeta no longer feared the barracuda, the shark, the swordfish. In the earlier months these had seemed to him so very swift. Now, with his long streamlined body, he could outstrip them with the greatest ease.

The mother was so proud. Peeta was as handsome as he was enormous. But he was not so enormous as to be ungainly. Sometimes at play or just to show off, he would go past the rocks like a silver flash. And she would smile. Yes, he had grown up, but he was still fond of play. And now he was so popular that his friends would not leave him alone. Every day he sported with the dolphins and corals and the anemones. And at night he came back to dream among the ferns.

Secretly his mother would be amused with his tales. Sometimes she stayed up just to hear them.

'Quiet,' she would say. 'Be quiet and go to sleep!' And he would gurgle teasingly among the rocks, and she would listen to his tales of the deep, about his pranks with the pretty corals and anemones. But about his new friend the moonfish Peeta said nothing. He had met her at the distant rocks.

As the days passed he thought of the moonfish more and more. It was she who he dreamed of when he lay among the ferns. There he saw her eyes again, sparkling like the crystal depths. There again he saw her tinted scales, gleaming like mirrors of silver. She was Iona, the Pride of the Sea. Thinking of her, Peeta became more and more wistful, until even his mother noticed and was puzzled. But Peeta kept silent. All his friends of the deep knew, though, and together they talked about it. They talked of how Peeta stared blindly into water, and how once he nearly swam in the way of the killer shark. They talked of Iona the Beautiful, and they envied her. For they knew what would be. And now the dolphins waited on the reefs in vain, and the corals, broken-hearted, murmured their low sad song.

Eventually Peeta spoke to his mother, for he wanted to go away. She wept because she too knew what would be. She asked who this Iona was, and Peeta was surprised. All the sea knew, he said; in the heights and in the depths; from the waters near the shore, to the waters of the limitless bounds; even the wonderful moon in the wind-water above the sea knew her, for they had played together and he had given his magic to her.

He said he would go away to the distant rocks and before many tides would return. Then would he bring back, he said, the greatest treasure of his days. He would bring to her his bride and her daughter – the Pride of the Sea.

The mother wept a little. For she realised that in this way Peeta was lost to her. And she knew she could not forbid this marriage even if she had wanted to. Therefore she warned him again of the open sea, for it was another of the terrible seasons of the great hands. And she told him of the ways to go. The ways which were difficult but safest. Then her heart lifted a little, for the marriage was good. As for the Monster of the Great Hands, the Providence which had guided Peeta so long would guide him still. She swam through the rocks looking around her. For now she had to prepare a home for her son and for the beautiful Iona, the Pride of the Sea.

The bay was deep and wide and the winds played on the face of the ocean. It was a beautiful month for fishing, although it was the mating season. In the mating season you did not catch fish plentifully, but if you were young and you went out with the sea calm and the breeze fresh, and with the sun lighting up the palm-fringed shore, sometimes you laughed aloud for the sheer joy of living and you didn't think of the fish at all.

Thus it had been with these fishermen riding the breakers. But now they cast out their nets with some enthusiasm because of the unexpected sight below. Halfway down, the water was foamy and rippling. The sign of fish.

Quickly they encircled the fish. They watched the leaden weight of the nets sink to the bottom. This would make their day. It came almost too easily. They watched each other, for it was unusual to come upon such a school of fish in the mating season.

Soon they were on shore hauling the catch in. They hauled as the fish struggled in the nets and the breakers chattered along the bay. They pulled and pulled, still amazed at their fortune, and when the nets dragged on sand and they could see the host of fins and tails flapping and lashing up the water, they were even more amazed and excited.

80

They dragged the catch right out onto the dry beach. There were hundreds of fish and crabs and corals. Even anemones.

'Look,' said one of the fishermen, pulling out a shiny flat fish from the living heap. Nearby a carite beat violently, gulping and leaping about on the sand. The fishermen were looking at the shiny fish.

'It's ages,' said the one with the fish, ' – years – since we brought in one of these.' He held the fish high. Its eyes gleamed as sparkling as the crystal depths and its scales were like mirrors of silver.

'Moonfish,' he said quietly. He was experienced and he knew it. 'Look at her! Pretty, eh?' he smiled. 'Boy, she is the Pride of the Sea!'

The carite nearby beat furiously.

# The Devils of Rose Hall

## Jean D'Costa

You don't have to believe this story. My uncle told it to me long ago; but my uncle didn't always tell the truth, so make up your own mind.

In 1920, Rose Hall Great House (the famous haunted Great House overlooking the blue Caribbean sea on the north coast of Jamaica) lay in ruins. No one had lived in the house for over fifty years. There it stood alone on the hills rising from the green cane fields. No other houses were ever built close to it. The manager's house and the labourers' cottages were as far away as possible, down near the beach, almost out of sight.

My uncle was a young fellow in those days, and he knew all the other young fellows hanging out around Falmouth and Montego Bay. They went bird-shooting and swimming together. But no one would stay long near that empty ruin.

The country people all around said that the devil lived there, and anyone who slept in the house would die violently and mysteriously during the night, or survive hopelessly insane.

But people did go into the house from time to time. My uncle did, for one, with some of his friends. They visited it in broad daylight, of course, and walked through the grand rooms thick with dust, down the narrow back stairs to the cellars where the infamous Annie Palmer used to practise black magic, and past the dark brown stain on the wall which, they say, is the blood of her last murdered husband.

No, Rose Hall wasn't a nice place at all, even in bright sunshine.

The windows were broken for the most part, and otherwise black with dust and grime. Cobwebs were everywhere, and hundreds of spiders of all sizes and colours were having a wonderful time raising large families and working industriously to bring them up. Rats lived there too: the kind of big, brown rats that stare at you like a prosecuting attorney, rats which wear seven-league boots and go down the wooden stairs 'clump – clump – CLUMP – *slither* – CRASSSSSH!' There were tribes and generations of these rats. And then there were mice, which chewed and chewed and chewed at goodness knows what behind the mahogany panelling in the bedrooms and dressing rooms, and carried on sudden conversations in high squeaks and whispers.

One thing you could be sure of: Rose Hall was not really *empty*, what with the rats and mice and spiders. And it was never really quiet either.

It sounded very still when you pushed open the creaking front door and stood in the weather-beaten hall. But soon you would hear furtive whispers, tiny footfalls, and the echo of noises which you had not made.

And of course all the furniture, and the carpets, paintings, lamps, chandeliers and curtains were long since gone. Most had been removed by the owners of Rose Hall Estate, but many pieces had been left behind to be looted by casual visitors as the years went by. What little remained had been destroyed by mice, damp and termites. The walls were dark with mildew and the whole house smelt old, cold, fusty and dank.

Now just around that time, says my uncle, a certain young Methodist minister came to live near to Falmouth. I shall call him the Rev. John MacGregor, but that was not his real name.

He was young and fiery and preached terrifying sermons. (So my uncle says, but *he* was never much of a churchgoer.)

The Rev. MacGregor preached all over the district, visiting villages in the hills and the small towns of St James and Trelawny. He soon had a reputation for being a fearless, outspoken man.

The young fellows of Falmouth got a bit annoyed with all this coming from someone no older than themselves. They decided to try out the Rev. MacGregor's famous courage.

On the first Sunday in every month, Rev. MacGregor did not prepare a sermon. Instead he put a closed box for suggestions beside the pulpit, and any note that he pulled out at random was made the text of that day's preaching. A

84

dangerous practice, I would have said, but the Rev. MacGregor liked to live dangerously.

On the first Sunday in November, the box was carefully emptied of all suggestions save one.

My uncle (who was in church on that day) says he doesn't know how it was done, because the box was locked and Rev. MacGregor had the only key tucked safely in the breast-pocket of his black suit.

The note was folded small, but he got it open and read out:

Dear Minister,

We have heard your courageous words spoken out against superstition and beliefs in black magic. Prove to us that such beliefs are false and groundless, as you claim. To do this, you can spend next Friday night, 13th November, alone in Rose Hall Great House.

Yours respectfully,
Some citizens of Falmouth.

Well they got their money's worth of sermon that day.

The Rev. MacGregor preached for three hours on voodoo, obeah, tea-leaf readings, palmistry, astrology and gambling. He mentioned idleness, gossip, bearing false witness against your neighbour, and the deceits of the world, the flesh and the devil.

'I take up this challenge,' he cried in ringing tones. 'I take it up with a happy heart for the sake of all this congregation. And when we meet again next Sunday, I will tell you of the folly of superstition and the deceits of Satan.'

The service ended and older members of the congregation flocked around him, begging him to disregard the challenge as the work of mischief-makers. Nobody had quite enough courage to come out and say that he would be in danger. Not after THAT sermon. But no one thought he should go. Some said that it was beneath his dignity, others that it was wasting valuable time, and everybody agreed that it was a nasty, unhealthy house where he would catch his death of cold or be bitten by a rat.

But the more they argued, the more stubborn he became, until he got angry and would hear no more.

'Since you are all so concerned about my well-being,' he said to the three most persistent parishioners, 'why don't you come with me on Friday night and see to it that I'm comfortable and happy? You won't have to *stay*, you know: I couldn't permit that,' he added wickedly.

They shut up and left him alone after that, but promised to go with him to Rose Hall at the appointed time.

Of course people gossiped like mad about it, and many more tried to dissuade him from going to Rose Hall, especially on Friday the 13th. The young fellows who were friends of my uncle did a lot to spread the story.

On Friday afternoon there was quite a crowd outside the minister's manse waiting to see him off in his buggy. Some looked scared, some were laughing, some were wringing their hands and conversing in whispers as if speaking of the dead. The only calm person was the Rev. MacGregor.

At about four o'clock the buggy moved off, for it was quite a long drive from Falmouth to Rose Hall, and the evenings were short.

At the bottom of the hill, just where the shaggy overgrown driveway began, the horse shied and refused to go any further. In any case the road became little better than a stony track, and the Rev. MacGregor was not willing to force his horse on such a treacherous path.

The friends who came with him helped him unpack the folding cot, the small suitcase with his nightgear and the little basket with his supper. They took everything up to the door, and as it was getting quite dark, one of them thoughtfully lit the lantern they had brought. Then they bade him a hasty goodnight with the excuse that it was getting late and they had a long drive back to Falmouth. No one set foot inside the house with him.

When they had disappeared down the hill, the Rev. John MacGregor stepped into the darkened hall and looked around for a place to spend the night.

He did not fancy the main hall with its rotting floor and open windows. The large banqueting room was little better. All the windows were broken and draughts of air stirred the cobwebs on the walls and made the yellow light of the lantern flicker.

He decided to try upstairs, and his feet sounded very loud and hollow on the wooden staircase as he went up, taking his time in case any of the boards had rotted through. Everything smelt damp and mouldy, and there was a furtive silence as if many ears were tuned to the noises of his intruding feet.

The bedroom at the back was the driest part of the house. The floor was less dusty and the windows were still undamaged. The last glow of the setting sun came from the windows to the west, filling the room with a deep ruby-red light in which the flame of the lantern glowed pale gold.

As he set up the camp bed with its blanket, the sun dipped behind the hills and the lantern shone out brightly in the thickening dark. He munched his egg and cheese sandwiches slowly, drank hot chocolate from a thermos flask, and watched from the window as the stars shone out brightly in the sky. He said his evening devotion silently, standing with his hands resting on the weather-beaten windowsill. Then he undressed, blew out the lantern and pulled the blanket over him.

He lay awake for a short while thinking over the events of the week and going over certain phrases in his sermon for the following Sunday. Then suddenly he fell asleep, with the creaking and whispering of the old house echoing in his ears. His last thought was to wonder sleepily how many hundred rats must be living in Rose Hall, and how many traps . . .

At fifteen minutes to midnight he was awakened from a deep sleep by a heavy knock on the door. He awoke as three loud knocks fell on his bedroom door; *thud, thud, thud.*

The sounds rang loud in the stillness. He realised in an instant that all the rustlings and creakings in the house had stopped. Everything was wrapped in a deathly hush. Even the wind was still outside.

'John MacGregor, come down to dinner!'

The voice rang out suddenly in the silence, authoritative and strong. He was not surprised that he did not know the voice. It must be some fellow-conspirator, possibly from Montego Bay. Well, he would show them.

He turned over and closed his eyes.

Nothing broke the stillness.

Then about five minutes later the knocking and the voice came again: *thud, thud, thud.*'

'John MacGregor, come down to dinner!'

The voice was louder this time.

His hot temper began to stir, but he pushed it to the back of his mind and lay still.

Five more minutes passed without a sound disturbing the awful silence inside and outside the house.

Then at five to twelve the rapping and the voice came again:

'*John MacGregor, come down to dinner!*'

He sprang from the cot in a flash of anger. This nonsense would soon be stopped.

He strode to the door, threw it open sharply, and fell back a step.

Light met him in the corridor. That was what he noticed first. And, almost unconsciously, the smells of polished wood, of distant flowers and of clean fresh air flowed over his senses as he stared at the stranger in the corridor. He was certainly no one he knew.

A tall, handsome man stood there, smiling faintly as he swept a courtly bow to John MacGregor standing in pyjamas and bare feet in the doorway. The stranger was dressed in full court dress of the late eighteenth century, with a coat of close-fitting black brocade, a waistcoat embroidered with pearls, elegant breeches of black satin and a single diamond flashing white fire from the foaming lace at his throat.

John MacGregor stared at him, speechless for once in his life.

The twisted smile deepened.

'Pray come below and join us, sir. Permit me to be your guide.'

And with an even deeper bow the stranger ushered the astonished clergyman out into the corridor and down the stairs.

The Rev. John MacGregor could not but stare about him.

A golden light came from clusters of candelabra on the walls, now gleaming white and hung with rich pictures between the curtained windows. Carpets glowed in dull sapphire, emerald and gold under his bare feet. Huge bowls of roses, orange myrtle with its desperate sweetness, and pale white tube lilies mingled their perfumes. The scents were overpowering.

Down, down they went in the deathly stillness, but as the stranger threw open the door to the banqueting room, somewhere in the depths of the house a clock chimed midnight in clear, musical tones.

And there before the Rev. John MacGregor's startled gaze stretched a magnificent banqueting table flanked by liveried servants waiting to serve the first course to eleven fine ladies and gentlemen. All were dressed in black and white like the host. Like him, their hair and faces were powdered deathly white, and on each painted cheek they wore a black satin patch in the shape of a skull.

He found himself held for a moment as eleven pairs of eyes gazed at him under the glare of the crystal chandelier hanging above them in a sparkle of lights.

Once more the host was bowing.

'Your seat is kept by me. Come now and dine with us!' The smile was echoed in the voice as the stranger trod noiselessly to the head of the table. John MacGregor found himself standing by an empty chair to the right of his host, and all the company followed him with their blank staring eyes as he took his stand there.

The striking of the clock had died away, and now the silence was deeper than ever. John MacGregor could hear his own breathing and even the beat of his heart as he stood still and wondered what to do.

The host was waiting courteously for him to be seated first, when John MacGregor suddenly seized the back of the chair hard, and looking slowly at all of the faces turned to him, he finally said in a low voice,

'I thank you for your kind and courteous request, and indeed I am honoured to be a guest at such a banquet as this. But before I may sit and dine with you, there is one thing which I must do.'

And he bowed his head with eyes firmly closed:

'JESUS, Thou name revered in Earth, and
Heaven, and Sea,
Before whom men and angels bow,
*But devils fear and flee*!'

He reeled back as from a blow.

A fearful screeching howl went up as the room
was plunged into pitch blackness. A wind rushed
past his face with a foul smell on it. There was a
hurrying, rushing noise like straw being thrown
into fire as the whole image vanished from his
eyes and he found himself utterly alone in the
damp, mouldy air of Rose Hall Great House.

Blinking a little, his eyes gradually became
accustomed to the dark as he felt his way back
up the stairs and so to bed.

Next morning found him fit and well as he
packed up his kit and came downstairs to await
the arrival of his friends and the buggy.

My uncle says that John MacGregor searched
the house carefully, and found no sign of anyone
anywhere. The only footprints in the dirt and
dust of the banqueting hall were those of his own
bare feet . . .

# The water woman and her lover

## Ralph Prince

It's an old Essequibo tale they used to tell in whispers. But even as they whispered the tale they were afraid the wind might blow their whisperings into the river where the water woman lived. They were afraid the water woman might hear their whisperings and return to haunt them as she had haunted her lover.

It's a strange story. Here it is from the beginning.

There was an old koker near Parika, through which water passed to and from the Essequibo river for drainage of the land in the area. On moonlit nights a naked woman was often seen sitting near the koker, with her back to the road and her face to the river.

She was a fair-skinned woman, and she had long, black, shiny hair rolling over her shoulders and down her back. Below her waist she was like a fish. When the moon was bright, especially at full moon time, you could see her sitting on the koker, combing her long, black, shiny hair. You could see very dimly just a part of her face – a

side view. But if you stepped nearer to get a closer look, she would disappear. Without even turning her head to see who was coming, she would plunge into the river with a splash and vanish. They called her Water Mamma.

People used to come from Salem, Tuschen, Naamryck and other parts of the east bank of the Essequibo river to see this mysterious creature. They would wait in the bush near the koker from early morning, and watch to see her rise from the river. But no matter how closely they watched, they would never see her when she came from the water. For a long time they would wait, and watch the koker bathed in moonlight. Then suddenly, as if she had sprung from nowhere, the water woman would appear sitting near the koker, completely naked, facing the river, and combing her long black hair.

There was a strong belief among the villagers in the area that riches would come to anyone who found Water Mamma's comb or a lock of her hair. So they used to stay awake all night at the koker, and then early in the morning, even before the sun rose, they would search around where she had sat combing her hair. But they never found anything. Only the water that had drained off her body remained behind – and also a strong fishy smell.

The old people said that after looking at Water Mamma or searching near the koker for her hair and her comb, you were always left feeling haunted and afraid. They told stories of people found sleeping, as if in a trance, while walking away from the koker. They warned that if a man watched her too long, and searched for her hair and her comb too often, he would dream about her. And if the man loved her and she loved him, she would haunt him in his dreams. And that would be the end of him, they said, because she was a creature of the devil.

These warnings did not frighten the younger and more adventurous men from the villages around. They kept coming from near and far to gaze at Water Mamma. After watching her and searching for her hair and her comb, they always had that haunted, fearful feeling. And many mornings, even as they walked away from the koker, they slept, as in a trance. But still they returned, night after night, to stare in wonder at that strange, mysterious woman.

At last something happened – something the old people had always said would happen – a man fell in love with the water woman. Some say he was from Salem. Some say he came from Naamryck. Others say he hailed from Parika, not far from the koker. Where he came from is not definitely known; but it is certain that he was a young man, tall and dark and big, with broad shoulders. His name was John, and they called him Big John because of his size.

When Big John had first heard of Water Mamma, he laughed and said she was a jumbie.

But as time went by, he heard so many strange things about her that he became curious. And so one moonlit night he went to the koker to look at the water woman.

He had waited for nearly an hour, and watched the moonlight shining on the koker and the river. His old doubts had returned and he was about to leave when he saw something strange, something that 'mek me head rise', as the old folks say when telling the story. He saw a naked woman sitting near the koker. A moment before, he had seen no one there. Then suddenly he saw this strange woman sitting in the moonlight and combing her long, black hair. It shone brightly in the moonlight.

Big John made a few steps towards her to see her more clearly. Then suddenly she was gone. Without even turning her head around to look at him, she plunged into the river with a big splash and vanished. Where he had seen her sitting, there was a pool of water. And there arose a strong fishy smell. A feeling of dread overcame him.

He then set out to get away from there. He tried to run but could only walk. And even as he began walking his steps were slow and his eyes were heavy with sleep. And that is the way he went home, walking and staggering, barely able to open his eyes now and then to see where he was going, walking and sleeping, as in a trance.

The next morning, when Big John awoke and

remembered what he had seen and experienced the night before, he became afraid. He vowed never to go back to the koker to look at the water woman. But that night the moon rose, flooding the land in silver, glistening in the trees, sparkling on the river. He became enchanted. His thoughts turned to the riverside and the strange woman combing her long, black hair.

And so later that night he stood near the koker waiting and watching for the strange woman to appear. Just like the night before, she appeared suddenly near the koker, combing her hair in the moonlight. Big John stepped towards her, but she plunged into the river and disappeared. And once again he had that feeling of dread, followed by drowsiness as he walked home.

This went on for several nights, with Big John becoming more and more fascinated as he watched the water woman combing her hair in the moonlight. After the third night, he no longer felt afraid, and he walked in the pool of water she had left behind. Sometimes he waited until morning and searched around for locks of her hair and her comb, but he never found them.

After a few months of this waiting and watching, Big John felt sad and lost. He had fallen in love with the strange woman. But he could not get near to her. And so he stopped going to the riverside to watch her.

When the moon had gone and the dark nights came back, he began to drop her from his mind. But in another month the moon returned, flooding the land in silver, gleaming in the trees, sparkling on the river, and he remembered the water woman, and he longed to see her combing her hair again.

And on the very night when the moon returned, he had a strange dream. He saw the water woman sitting near the koker, combing her long, black hair shining in the moonlight. She sat with her back to the river and her face full towards him. As she combed her hair, she smiled at him, enchanting him with her beauty. He stepped forward to get a closer look, but she did not move. And so at last he saw her clearly, her bright eyes, her lovely face, her teeth sparkling as she smiled, and her body below her waist tapered off like a fish. She was the most beautiful creature he had ever seen.

He stretched out his hands to touch her, and she gave him her comb and said, 'Take this to remember me by.'

Then she jumped into the river and disappeared.

When he awoke the next morning, he remembered the dream. He felt happy as he told his friends what he had seen in the dream. But they were afraid for him, and they warned him:

'Is haunt she hauntin' you.'

'She goin' mek you dream an' dream till you don' know wha' to do wid yourself.'

'When she ready she goin' do wha' she like wid you.'

'Big John, you better watch yourself wid de water woman.'

'De water woman goin' haunt you to de en'.'

These warnings made Big John laugh, and he told them:

'She can' do me anyt'ing in a dream.'

But they warned him again:

'You forget 'bout de water woman, but she don' forget 'bout you.'

'Is you start it when you watch she so much at de koker.'

'Now you 'rouse she an' she want you. Da is de story now, she want you.'

Big John laughed off these warnings and told them that nothing was going to happen to him as nothing could come from a dream.

But later that day he saw something strange. It made him shiver with dread. On the floor near his bed was a comb. He could not believe his eyes. It looked very much like the comb the water woman had given to him in the dream. He wondered how a comb he had seen in a dream could get into his room.

When he told his friends about finding the comb they said:

'Is bes' for you to go 'way from here.'

'Is you start it when you watch she so much at de koker.'

That night he had another dream. In this

dream he saw the water woman sitting in the moonlight. He stepped even closer to her than before, and she smiled at him.

For the first time since he had seen her, she was not combing her hair, and she had no comb in her hand. She pulled out a few strands of her hair and gave them to him and said, 'Keep these to remember me by.' And he took them in his hands and smiled at her. In another instant she was gone with a splash into the river.

The next morning Big John awoke with a smile as he remembered the dream. But as he sat up in the bed he found himself with a few strands of hair in his hands. His eyes opened wide in surprise. It was only then that he realised that he was getting caught up in something strange.

And so the dreams went on, night after night. They became like magnets drawing Big John to bed early every night, and holding him fast in sleep till morning. They no longer made him feel afraid on awakening.

In one dream, the water woman gave him a conch shell. On awakening the next morning he found sand on his bed and grains of sand in both hands. One night he dreamt that he and the water woman played along the river bank splashing each other with water. The next morning he found his bed wet, and water plashed all over the room.

Big John told his friends about these dreams, and they warned him that the water woman had him under a spell. They were right. He kept on dreaming about her night after night.

Then came his last dream. The water woman stood by the riverside holding a large bundle to her bosom. She smiled and said:

'You have my comb and strands of my hair. I have given you other little gifts to remember me by. Tonight I shall give you money to make you rich. If you keep it a secret, you will stay on earth and enjoy it. If you do not keep it a secret, you must come with me and be my lover for ever.'

She hurled the bundle to him, and then jumped into the river and was gone.

When Big John awoke the next morning, he found the floor of the room covered with tens of thousands of five-dollar bills, piled up high in heaps. It took him a long time to gather them and count them. It was a vast fortune.

Big John was too excited to keep the news about the dream and the fortune it had brought him. He went around the village and told some of his closest friends about it. When they went with him to his house and saw those great piles of money, their eyes bulged and their mouths opened wide in amazement.

Then they made a wild scramble for it. They fought among themselves all that afternoon for the money. Some of them got away with little fortunes. Some ran away with their pockets bulging with notes. Others were left with notes that got torn up in the scrambling and fighting.

Big John himself was beaten by the others and got nothing. They ran away and left him.

What happened to Big John after that no one knows. Some say he dreamed again of the water woman that night and she took him away in the dream. Some say he went to the koker several nights to look for her but never found her, and so he drowned himself in the river. Others say that the water woman sent her water people for him, and they took him to live with her in her home at the bottom of the river.

But if you go down to the koker near Parika on any night of the full moon, you will see the water woman sitting with her back to the road and her face to the river, combing her long, black, shiny hair in the moonlight. You will also see a tall, big man with broad shoulders standing close beside her.

# Jeffie Lemmington and me

## Merle Hodge

I was seven and I had thought that snow was like cotton wool, so I had always wondered how the children in books made snowmen stand up without the breeze blowing them away.

When my mother woke me up one morning, she said, 'There's snow, darling, come and see!'

We stood at the window looking down. The tops of the parked cars were covered with thick white hair, as though they had grown old in the night. The pavement was covered with it, too, and the roof – the long row of joined-together roofs – of the opposite side of the street, everything. It was very mysterious. A giant had come and quietly laid his fluffy white towel down over the whole street and vanished again.

My mother was holding me. 'Pretty, eh?' she said. I did not answer. Instead I squirmed with shyness. I was shy of my mother. I did not know my mother, I did not know my father, and – I did not trust the little boy they had with them who did not talk like me and didn't seem to feel cold, who they said was my little brother.

I had looked forward to seeing my little brother. When I was going to take the plane, Granny had given me a paperbag full of sweets to bring for him. And he had sniffed and nibbled at them, screwing up his face, and handed them back to my mother.

In the night when I was falling asleep, or when I woke up in the middle of the night, then this place seemed to be a dream that I was having. It was always close and dark here, as in a dream, and there was no midday; the whole day was the same colour. And you could never just scamper out through the front door if you felt like it, you had first to pile on all those clothes that made you feel heavier than when you had got soaked in the rain.

But when I was up and about, then it was Granny and Uncle Nello who seemed to be tucked away in a dream somewhere, or in some bright yellow storybook.

Granny was both sad and happy when they'd written and said that I could go to them now. Happy for me because at last I was going Up There. They were rather put out when I announced that I wasn't going anywhere. I hadn't the slightest interest in my mother and father – only when I got parcels from them with sweets and toys; but when I had gobbled up the sweets and broken the toys or exchanged them for things my friends had, then I forgot about my mother and father until the next parcel came.

But I didn't mind going Up There to have a look at this little brother who seemed to have crept into the world behind my back, for Granny and Uncle Nello said that I had never seen him. (They also said that I *had* seen my mother and father and that they had seen me, but I knew they were only fooling me.)

And now I had come to this uncomfortable place, and I had seen my little brother, and now I was ready to go back to Granny and Uncle Nello.

We put on all our clothes, my mother and I, and set out for school. But . . . snow was crunchy to walk on, like biscuit crumbs, not a bit like cotton wool! My mother was picking her way carefully along, and I soon discovered why. For we had made only a few steps when my shoes played a trick on me and I sat down in the snow. It was hard, and I stayed sitting and bellowed at the top of my voice. This was enough. I wanted to go home to Granny and Uncle Nello. Enough of this foolish place.

Every day my mother took me to school and came and fetched me in the afternoon. Even when I knew the way myself. I wanted to walk with Jeffie Lemmington. We lived on the same street. And besides, hardly anyone else's mother brought them to school and came to fetch them like babies. So on afternoons when I came through the school gates and out of the corner of my eye had checked to see that my mother was standing there, I then ignored her, and walked a little way behind her all the way home.

But after a while she stopped coming and then Jeffie Lemmington and I made our joyful way together to and from school. We walked along the tops of little garden walls, our arms cutting through the air like windmills; we played hide-and-seek in and out of the crowd along the street that was always full of people; when we had to cross the road, we stood on the pavement and held hands, and he looked to the left and I looked to the right, and then we raced over; we fished a tin can out of a dustbin and kicked it all the way home, enjoying the delightful noise it made on the concrete. And we played together at school, too, Jeffie Lemmington and me. When Jeffie Lemmington and I were playing together, then I almost forgot that I didn't like this place and wanted to go back to Granny and Uncle Nello.

One morning, Jeffie Lemmington did not meet me at our gate and I set out alone. Then I saw him a little way ahead of me and called happily to him as I charged down the street. But when I caught up with him, he looked at me miserably. 'My mum says I'm not to play with you,' he said, kicking a stone.

'Why?' I asked in astonishment.

'Because she says you prob'ly smell and you'll give me lice.'

'What is lice?'

His face brightened for a moment. 'Don' you know what lice is?' he said, sticking his chest out. 'Haw, I've 'ad lice heaps of times!'

Lice I pictured as some tempting dessert that wasn't really too good for you. His face fell again and we walked along thinking, trying to puzzle the whole thing out.

At recreation time we did not play, we stood near to each other on the playground with our hands in our pockets, each sadly kicking at a blade of grass or spinning slowly on one heel. Then suddenly Jeffie Lemmington stood stock still. 'I know what!' he said, running towards me. 'I'll take you to my mum so she can smell you, and when she smells you don't smell of anything, then we can play!' We hugged each other and danced round and round.

We could not wait for that schoolday to end. In the classroom we looked at each other every now and then and smiled. When school was over we burst out of the gates, almost dragging each other along by the hand as we pelted down the road.

Jeffie Lemmington was ringing the doorbell, still gripping my hand. A lady opened the door, smiling. But suddenly her mouth gasped like a fish's and her eyes grew wide, then her eyes got small and her mouth clamped together hard and angry, and I was terrified. And the next thing I knew Jeffie Lemmington's hand was pulled from mine and he was disappearing head first through the door by no will of his own, and BRAM I was standing in front of a dirty cream door in a cold passage in a strange house.

I dashed down the stairs as fast as my legs could carry me and ran all the way home, crying.

My mother said, with a strange look on her face, well that was that, I couldn't play with *him* any longer; maybe the best thing to do would be to find a little boy just like me to play with; there were some little boys like me at the school, weren't there? But Jeffie Lemmington *was* just like me! He was seven and he was going to be a footballer and he hated milk. But my mother clamped her mouth together and wouldn't say a word more.

I threw a tantrum. If I couldn't play with my friend Jeffie Lemmington, then I wasn't staying in this place any longer; I was going home. My little brother stood with his thumb in his mouth and stared, impressed, as I bravely kicked and writhed and roared. I made a face at him and he stepped back.

The next day, Jeffie Lemmington and I walked to school on opposite sides of the street. Every now and then we peeped sideways at each other; every time we came to a corner, each took a quick look to see that the other was crossing safely.

At recreation time we were standing near to each other again, kicking at pebbles, when I had an idea this time: 'Let's run away!'

What I had in mind was running away to Granny and Uncle Nello. Jeffie Lemmington said that we would run away to a farm and be farm-hands, shearing sheep and slaughtering cows, until we were older, then we'd become footballers, because they didn't take little boys of seven to be footballers. The idea wasn't a bad one, and at any rate I would go along with it until I could get back to Granny and Uncle Nello.

We would get on the train, and when we had been on the train long enough then we'd be in the country, where farms were, said Jeffie Lemmington. He knew, he'd been to the country once, to a farm.

We did not shoot out of the school gates as we had done the day before. But we held hands even more tightly than the day before. Looking neither right nor left, nor, above all, at each other, we set off down the road. At the corner where we usually crossed over, we firmly turned right instead, and after we had gone a few steps, we could look at each other and smile happily, and then break into a run.

Down in the Underground the escalators were a temptation, we *had* to ride on them for a bit. We rode up and down and backwards on the escalators until suddenly a million people were hurrying down the passage, clattering with their feet, and they filled up the escalator and there were still more coming; so we decided to continue on our way to the country.

And there wasn't much else we could do, for now we were being sucked along in a kind of wave, like the time when the sea grabbed me and was dragging me away when I was little, but Uncle Nello had been there to pull me out; and Jeffie

113

Lemmington was terrified, too, for he held on to me as we were carried forward.

But all of a sudden the crowd came loose and we were free. We were on the train platform. We wanted to go home.

'Fun, ain't it?' squeaked Jeffie Lemmington.

'Yes, fun, ain't it?' I squeaked in agreement. A fearful thundering – the train never thundered so when we were down in the Underground with our mothers – and the giant centipede rushed in.

We were pushed into it and we clutched each other again. When the doors slid shut and locked us away, Jeffie Lemmington and I were standing pressed tightly together stomach to stomach, so that we had to take turns drawing breath.

We travelled like this for a long time, shaken to and fro, not saying a word, until the train began to empty itself. 'I think the next stop's the country,' came Jeffie Lemmington's frightened voice.

We followed some people off the train and up the stairs, walking quietly behind them so they wouldn't notice. We were oozing through a small space in a barrier, and just as we escaped to the other side a voice called out sharply:

'Tickets! You two! Come back here!'

'Run!' said Jeffie Lemmington; and we ran.

But at the door Jeffie Lemmington stood stock still and looked as if he was going to cry. He was staring about. 'But this isn't the country!' he said.

We had no idea how long we had been walking in the streets. But it was dark now, and we were cold. There was food in lighted windows. We had not spoken for a long time. We were too frightened. We were more frightened than we were hungry, or tired, or cold. Our mothers would never find us, and what was going to become of us? I thought of my mother and father and little brother sitting eating, indoors, in the warm. How dare they! – when I was not there. Sometimes people looked at us curiously.

Suddenly Jeffie Lemmington sat down, in the middle of the pavement, and bawled. Right away I dropped down beside him and did the same. We sat on the pavement side by side and bellowed at the tops of our voices. People passing stopped and stood around us, looking as if they were not sure what they should do; and then a lady bent down and asked us where we lived.

We don't really remember the ride in the police car, because by then we were fast asleep, but all the other boys think we do. We've told them how they let us blow the siren and make the light on top flash as we tore through the streets, and other cars had to move aside as we raced along . . . . All we really remember is the lady taking us to her house and giving us dinner; and she tried to give us milk, and we fell asleep.

And then us in the newspaper. "Ow do we know it's you?' said George Tiller, but he was only

115

jealous. Of course he is right, maybe; if you didn't know, you'd think it was just some policemen and my mother and Jeffie Lemmington's mum holding two bundles with legs and looking right silly, laughing like twits.

And my mother has told *every*body, a million times (if you knew my mother, you'd expect her to tell one story a million times), how funny it was, when the policemen came in with the two bundles in blankets how they each rushed and grabbed one, and how the two bundles were exactly the same size and only our shoes and socks were showing, black shoes and grey socks with a green stripe – and if you knew my mother, you'd expect her to get the wrong bundle, and so did Jeffie Lemmington's mum. So that's why they're all laughing in the picture like twits. I wish they'd turned us around so everybody could see it *was* us, Jeffie Lemmington and me.

# My mother

## Velma Pollard

For Marjorie

The Lexington Avenue train raced into Fourteenth Street station like a runaway horse and
miraculously came to a stop; belching forth such
an army of fast-moving bodies that I flattened
myself against the stair-rails in sheer terror. But
I survived, and after the first flight of stairs, stood
near a tiny candyshop in the station, to let them
all pass.

I stared, but only at the blacks – the strangers
whom this heartless machine had rushed out of
Harlem, out of the safety of the familiar 125th
Street and into this alien city; to dingy stores
and tiny disorganised offices or to other vague
connections: Canarsie, Long Island, Jamaica, etc.
They were all running, in some way or other –
in careless abandon or in crisp, short, overbred
paces; the women's girdles and eventually their
coats, controlling the obviousness of the movement; the men's coat tails flapping at the inevi-
table slit below the rump.

The men, whether they were briefcase types
or lunch-pan types, all wore little hats with
short brims. It was a cold morning. In New

118

York twenty-three degrees is considered cold. The women didn't need hats. Cheap, curly wigs hugged their temples protecting their black youthfulness and hiding their kinky strands. Fifty acknowledging thirty needs a wig. For some reason the real hairline tells a story even when it is dyed black. And here the merciful cold allowed for the constant sweater or the little scarf that covers the telltale neck.

Everybody was running and everybody looked frightened. But you could see that all this had become natural. This speed was now normal and because they couldn't see their own frightened faces, they couldn't recognise their fright. When you answer long enough to a name that for one reason or another is wrong, and when you live long enough with a face that is always wrong, a frightened look grows on you and becomes an inseparable part of you. I looked at them and became numb with a kind of nameless grief. For I had seen my mother for the first time in all those tense women's faces, in all those heads hiding their age and gentleness beneath the black, curly wigs.

The little journey was a ritual. Very early, the first or second Saturday morning of the month, my Grandmother and I would walk to Anne's Ridge and get in the line at the bank. I would sign my name on the money order made out to me and we would soon move from the Foreign

Exchange line to the Savings line. I never knew how much money came, for the exchange from dollars to pounds was too much for me to handle; and I never knew how much was saved. But I always felt, one Saturday every month, that we were rich.

Sometimes we stopped in the big Anne's Ridge stores in town and bought a new plate or two, sometimes dress material and v-e-r-y occasionally, shoes. Then we stopped in the market for the few things Gran didn't plant and Mass Nathan's shop didn't stock.

The journey home was less pleasant. I never ever noticed the hills on the way back; not because they were so much less green but because it took all my energy to think up little stories to help me block out Gran's monthly lecture. It always had to do with ingratitude. I'm not sure now how she knew the extent of my ingratitude long before I even understood the concept of gratitude. It had to do with the faithfulness of her daughter working hard in America to support me so I could 'come to something' and my not trying to show thanks. I was no great writer; but Gran saw to it that I scratched something on an airletter form to my mother every month and that something always included thanks for the money.

Gran never made it clear in what non-verbal ways I should express this thanks. I had to do well at school; but the teachers had a sort of fool-proof mechanism for assuring that – those were the days of the rod and I meant to be a poor customer for that. So school was okay. But the guidelines at home were less clear. An action that one day was a sign of ingratitude was, next day, a normal action. It seems that the assessment of my behaviour was a very arbitrary and subjective exercise and depended partly on Gran's moods.

Now I understand what Gran's dilemma was like. She herself did not know what she had to produce from the raw material she was given if her daughter's sacrifice was not to be meaningless. She had been set a great task and she was going to acquit herself manfully at all costs; but she was swimming in strange waters. And her daughter could only work and send money; she couldn't offer guidelines either – only vague hints like the necessity for me to speak properly, however that should be.

Every year we expected my mother home on vacation, and every year she wrote that she was sorry she couldn't make it. But she always sent, as if to represent her, a large, round box that people insisted on calling a barrel. It was full of used clothes of all sorts, obviously chosen with little regard for my size or my grandmother's size. I never went to the collecting ceremony. This involved a trip to Kingston and endless red tape. I merely waited at the gate till the bus turned the curve, gave its two honks and slid along the loose stones to a halt to let my grandmother out. Then the sideman would roll the barrel along the top of the bus and shove it to his comrade. Immediately the bus would honk again and move on.

Nothing smelt exactly like my mother's boxes. It was a smell compounded from sweat and mustiness and black poverty inheriting white cast-offs. I still remember one of those dresses from the box. With today's eyes, I can see that it was a woman's frock; a short woman's voile frock for cocktail parties or an important lunch. And I was nine or ten then. But I wore it with pride, first to the Sunday School Christmas concert and then to numerous 'social' events thereafter. And even now, that low-slung waist or anything resting lightly on the hips has particular charm for me whether or not the beholder's eye shares my judgement . . . . There were blouses and shoes and hats; something to fit almost every one in my grandmother's endless chronicle of cousins. We accepted our ill-fitting fits and wore them with surprising confidence.

Every year we expected my mother home on vacation. But she never came. The year I was in Third Form they flew her body home. I hadn't heard that she was ill. I felt for months afterwards that my very last letter should have said something different, something more; should have shown more gratitude than the others. But I could not possibly have known that it would be the last.

When the coffin arrived, it was clear that nobody from Jamaica had touched that coffin. Sam Isaacs may have kept it a few days but that was all. The whole thing was foreign – large, heavy, silvery, straight from the USA. And when they opened the lid in the church, so she could lie in state and everybody could look and cry, it was clear that my mother too had been untouched by local hands. She had come straight from the USA.

When my mother left Jamaica I couldn't have been more than five or six, so any memory I had of her was either very vague or very clear and original – carved out of my own imagination with patterns all mixed up of other people's mothers and of those impersonal clothes in the annual barrel. The woman in the coffin was not my mother. The woman in the purple dress and black shoes (I didn't even know they buried people in shoes), the highly powdered face, framed by jet black curls and covered lightly with a mantilla, was not like any of the several images I had traced.

The funeral couldn't be our funeral. It was a spectacle. I don't suppose more than half the people there had actually known my mother. But it was a Sunday and the whole week that had elapsed between the news of her death and the actual funeral made it possible for people from far and near to make the trip to our village. Those who were from surrounding districts but had jobs in the city used one stone to kill two birds – visit

123

the old folks at home, and come up to 'Miss Angie daughter funeral'.

It wasn't our funeral. It was a spectacle.

The afternoon was hot; inside the church was hotter. Outside, I stood as far as I could from the grave and watched several of them pointing at me, their eyes full of tears: 'Dats de little one she lef wid Miss Angie.' Near to me was a woman in a fur hat, close fitting, with a ribbon at the side. She wore a dress of the same yellow gold as the hat, and long earrings, costume jewellery, of the same yellow gold.

I could hear the trembling voices from the grave –

> 'I know not, O, I know not,
> What joys await us there . . .'

and fur hat, beside me, trying to outdo them so her friend could hear her.

'A didn' know ar but a see de face; is fat kill ar noh?' (My mother was rather busty but that was as far as the fat went.)

She didn't wait for an answer but continued: 'A nevva see one of dese deads that come back from Englan' yet.' (No one had taken the trouble to tell her it was America, not England.)

'But de reason why a come to see ar is becaaz I was dere meself an' a always say ef a ded, dey mus sen me back. Is now a see ow a woulda look! But teng Gad a lucky a come back pon me own steam . . . . An' you see dis big finneral shi have?

She wouldn't have get it in Englan' you know. Since one o'clock she woulda gaan an' if they cremate ar, while we drinking a cuppa tea, she bunnin'.'

'Wat?' asked her audience at last. 'Deh gives tea? An' peeple siddung?'

'Man, deh put dem in someting like a oven, an' by de time we jus' drink de tea, you get de ashes an' you gaan . . .'

They had stopped singing about my mother's joys; the slow heavy dirge was now 'Abide with Me' sung with the Baptist rhythm, sad and slow, though I hardly think it is possible for that particular song to be anything but sad and slow, Baptist or no Baptist. I looked towards the crowd. They were supporting my Grandmother. I knew she wasn't screaming. She was never given to screaming. She was just shaking as great sobs shook her body and her hands seemed to hold up her stomach. It was pointless my trying to comfort her; they wouldn't let me. Two old women were holding her, Miss Emma, her good friend, and Cousin Jean, who was more like a sister than a cousin.

The next day I went alone to my mother's grave to push my own little bottle with maidenhair fern into the soft, red earth. When all their great wreaths with purple American ribbons had long faded, my maidenhair fern started to grow.

I had never known my mother. I had known her money and her barrels and my grandmother's

respect for her. I had not wept at her funeral.
But that morning, in the subway station at
Fourteenth Street, in the middle of nowhere,
in the midst of a certain timelessness, I wept for
her, unashamedly, and for the peace at Anne's
Ridge that she never came back to know, after
the constant madness, after the constant terror of
all the Fourteenth Street subway stations in that
horrifying workhouse.

I saw my tears water the maidenhair fern on
her grave to a lush and green luxuriance. I was
glad I was a guest in the great USA and a guest
didn't need a wig. I would take no barrels home
with me. I saw my mother's ancient grave covered
again with its large and gaudy wreaths. Like the
mad old man in Brooklyn, I lifted from a hundred
imaginary heads, a hundred black and curly wigs
and laid them all on the ancient grave. And I laid
with them all the last shapeless, ill-fitting clothes
from the last barrel. The last of the women had
hurried away. I wept for my mother. But I
rejoiced that the maidenhair fern was lush and
that we had no longer need for gaudy wreaths.

# The legend of Talon

## Calvin Watson

Long before the three men could even begin to make out his figure, he saw them approaching. Even in the pallid moonlight his eyesight was exceptional.

Three of them were walking abreast, about twenty yards behind the fourth man. He could sense that something was about to happen, so he darted behind the embankment to watch.

He was right. By the time the man in front came alongside where he was hiding, the other three who had silently and efficiently closed the gap, sprang at the man. But he was apparently expecting the attack: he half-turned as the men pounced, moving to one side and away from them with disdainful ease.

The men – still acting as one – came to an abrupt stop. Undaunted however, the one in the middle pulled out a gun. His companions pulled ratchet knives.

'Awright, Babylon Bwoy, hand over the irons.' The one with the gun spoke in a menacing tone.

He saw the blurring movement from 'Babylon'. He saw the flash of bright blue light. He heard the air rent with the explosion. He saw the man holding the gun staggering backwards and then falling! He heard the high-pitched scream rising from the lungs of the falling man! He saw the other two, in confusion, throwing away their knives and dashing down the road!

He saw it all, but he did not believe it! No other man could have handled a gun that way!

He saw the man running after the fleeing men: suddenly the man dropped to one knee, took aim and fired again. The man must be mad! In the dim moonlight, could the man's sight be that good? And as for his accuracy . . .!

He could still see the running men. One of them stumbled and fell. The man fired again, and the second man went down. The man rose from his knees and returned to where the first man lay groaning on the road.

'Jesus in Heaven – !' He was mortified and astonished. Could a man be *that* good? What eyesight! What accuracy! What body movement . . .! Yes, what movement! The man could not be human: he had to be a demon from the heat of hell. He had moved as if no physical movement was impossible for him, such smooth flowing motion, yet precise and firm.

In all his forty five years he had never seen anyone move with such natural grace, such perfect timing and coordinated precision as to make every gesture effortless. It was as people say, pure poetry in motion.

He stepped from the bushes and cleared his throat to warn the man of his approach.

The man looked over his shoulder at him indifferently.

'Goodnight, officer,' he addressed the man. 'I saw everything. Yes, sir! This is one time that they cannot claim police brutality. Why, officer, if you were not here they would have killed me! That's why I had to hide myself.'

The man looked at him with bored contempt. Yet when he spoke, his voice was hard and even, no trace of heavy breathing to show his recent activities.

'No, everything is all right, man. These guys can't give no trouble.'

He noted that the man was firm and strong, but with nothing extraordinary about him to reveal the fact that he could move at incredible speed.

'I must congratulate you, officer, on the speedy and efficient way that you dealt with these criminals. You will have to give me your name, for I must write a letter to the Commissioner, recommending that you be promoted. Your fellow policemen must be proud of you.'

'Never get the chance to show it to them,' the man answered looking down indifferently at the groaning man.

'What about his friends down the road?'

'Nothing much. Just shot them in the leg.' A note of impatience crept into his voice. Holy angel. The man was not human after all. In such poor visibility, and at such a distance, he had aimed and shot the men where he wanted.

'Hell, officer, you must be the greatest thing in the entire Constabulary Force.' His voice was tinged with awe and respect that he had shown to no other man in memory.

'No, you jus' jokin', old man.'

Old. The policeman had called him old. The realisation hit him like a thunderbolt. Did the policeman know who he was? How would the policeman react if he knew that he too had a gun on him, and that he could have moved in the same precise manner and would have achieved the same result?

He dazedly wished the policeman goodnight and walked home in a sleepwalking trance. His spirits were crushed. The man said he was old. Old at forty-five! The policeman must be joking. Wait until he reached forty-five and see if he would be calling himself old then!

He locked the doors of the sprawling comfortable house where he lived alone. In his bedroom, he turned on the lights, took his gun and placed it on the bed. He checked his features in the mirror. His face was still hard, no baggy puffs around the eyes, no creases anywhere at all, no sagging jello-jumping jowls. Good. A sprinkling of grey hairs, yes, but what did that prove? Men years younger had more grey hairs.

He turned his side to the mirror and admired his reflection. Still hard, lean and tall. He steadied his hand before the mirror. No nervous shaking.

He was still in the superb condition of twenty-five years ago.

Suddenly he stiffened, pivoted, and leapt to the ceiling, pushing back the trap door, landing back on his toes with another gun in his hand, as light as a cat. No one could surprise him at his home – he was too careful for that!

He put the gun in his waistband, faced his image in the mirror and flexed his muscles, taking a deep breath at the same time. Then he allowed his body to go limp. Only his shirt pocket jerked lightly to his heartbeat.

His gun was in his hand in a flash! Just a neat twinkling movement – the same as the policeman's. He was still incredibly fast, he grinned in gleeful satisfaction. Everything was still there. Stupid little baby boy, amateur policeman calling him old! Old men do not do those things.

The police boy should have seen what he just did. His stupid little eyes would pop out and roll on the floor like a pair of dice.

Where was the little amateur when he was the scourge of the villages neighbouring on Elbows Bend in his younger days? Come to think of it, he must have broken into more houses, from country to Kingston, than the number of days the boy had spent in the Force. He had stolen more money than the stupid little boy would ever earn in his life, and he had raped more women than he would ever say hello to.

Let the little boy go back to places like

Blackfields, Litchens, Walnut Grove and ask about the housebreaking specialist of two decades gone, and watch the women tremble with fear and the men scowl with rage.

Let him ask from Kingston to Spanish Town, and he would hear of the man who moved like a supernatural being. He could even ask some of the older heads in the Force. They would tell him of the one who leaps from rooftops with the light, smooth agility of a cat. He must have heard of the one who shoots with such uncanny accuracy that time and time again they were left astounded. Yes, anyone could tell him of that one, chased by police and citizens alike, but never caught.

He was the most competent housebreaker in the business. From the time when he had started it as a joke with the toy gun, he had never looked back and he had never done anything else. He was never enticed by the lure of big business places. They had too many sophisticated weapons and gadgets to trap a man. Houses were not that fortified. An occasional bad dog or a scared occupant with an old rusting gun, which he had no idea how to operate in the first place, were about all the hazards he encountered.

Well, it would not be a bad idea to meet the policeman again on another lonely night. Yes, he would do it just as soon as he took care of that house in Gregory Park. The people might return at any time now.

After that, he would seek out the policeman

and astound him with the accuracy of an old man. Strange how one always had to concentrate on the fast draw when one makes the gun a constant companion. One's life could depend on it, just as on a partner.

His mind instantly recalled the days when he used to work with partners. Of all his partners, Shorty and Curly were the better ones. Shorty, however, had no discipline and that had brought about his downfall. They had broken into a home where Shorty discovered the liquor and proceeded to drink himself into a stupor. When the police surprised them, Shorty did not even know himself.

Curly was different. A strong disciplinarian, but too ambitious. He considered housebreaking to be 'petty thieving' and wanted to move up to 'where the real money was'.

So many had fallen by the wayside because they had allowed their ambition to overrule their good sense. Curly was one who had neither the talent nor the decency to be a self-respecting pickpocket, yet he wanted to do bank jobs.

He had resisted Curly, and that had brought a silent rift between them. It was quite clear to him that they would be parting company on rather violent terms and so he planned for the looming confrontation. Not even the householder who shot Curly to death realised that Curly had fallen into a well-laid trap.

He reached the house in Gregory Park at about

eleven at night. It was dark and silent. The moon was under a cloud. Out of the silvery darkness a dog came silently at him. But he was alert.

He spun away in a neat dancing step and shot the animal once in the head as it hurtled by. The gun, muffled by the silencer, made a popping sound. The dog spun and fell with a feeble, dying yelp.

Then above the chirping of the crickets he heard the faint unmistakable click of a gun. Fumbling amateur police. Another occupational hazard, but he would take care of it. He quickly slipped through the wire fence at the back of the house and sprinted off into the meadowland.

He heard shouts then, and a bullet buzzed into a tree a yard to his right. He chuckled mirthlessly. It would be the same story all over again. He would run them all into the ground with the majority giving up after a mile or so. A few obstinate ones would continue for another mile, then they too would give up.

He ran about three miles that night, the extra mile added just for the exercise and to prove to himself that he was not old. His journey took him through meadowlands, pastures and a cane field. At the end of the cane field he came abruptly to a one-room cottage, and, as he passed, he noted that an old man was looking at him through a window. Three chains away he glanced back and saw that the old man was standing at the door, still watching him.

He stopped then. His breath was still almost even. A running man in the night, especially in these lonely parts, was enough to arouse anyone's curiosity, but the old man was more than curious. What if the police checked with the old man the following day? He may just have seen too much.

He took out his gun and checked it. Pity the old man's time had come. '"The time has come", the Walrus said.' How that line had stuck in his memory ever since he was about to assault a house when he overheard a girl reading those lines from a book. How appropriate it was. The time had come for that house. The time had come for the old man. He tucked the gun back into his waist and began to walk towards the house.

Suddenly he jerked to a stop. The young policeman was standing fifteen metres away from him. He felt his heart beating faster.

'Ha, ha, officer, we always seem to meet when I'm on my nightly strolls.' His voice and laughter were unconvincing, he knew that, but where did the man materialise from? It was enough to rattle a man's teeth.

'And quite a long stroll it was too, man. Thought you would never stop. Been behind you all the way from down Gregory Park way.'

He felt the coldness of fear leaping up in his bowels, and his hands trembled. How much did the man know? Was that the way it had to go, after years of eluding even the superintendents? A mere wisp of an amateur constable, baby-faced and still new, had to be the one to take him in? Not in any way.

'Officer, I think there must be some mistake. I don't know what you're talking about. I am a respectable man, known throughout Kingston, St Andrew and St Catherine.'

'. . . And Blackfields, Litchens and Elbows Bend. You forget those, man. You really have come a long way, but at last, no matter how long the road is, there must be an end to it. What do you say about that, Talon?

He found himself reeling but realised that the sensation was only in his mind. No one had called him Talon for about twenty years, not since he left Elbows Bend for Kingston, cultivated respectability, but continued his work.

So the boy knew who he was! That maybe was the reason why he was standing there looking so confident, waiting . . . like a blasted ghost.

'So what are you doing to do about it, now that we know one another?'

'I know you, but you don't know me. Back in Elbows Bend, they say that you were so fast with a gun that no eye could follow you. I want to see if it is true, man.'

So that was it?

'What else did they say about me?'

Stall for time. Not only were the hands shaking but the palms were sweating. He could not pull his gun with a wet hand. He surely would miss, or the thing would spin from his hand.

'They say that you are the best housebreaker that there ever was, and that you rape with speed and ease. Night after night, the older men would tell us youngsters about the fantastic Talon, the man who could jump from rooftops, melt into darkness, and even shoot three policemen with one bullet. Many more fables, and it was a long time before I realised that it was all a big fable. But, back there, Talon is a legend. Talon is the man named after the cat.'

He remembered the days with the toy gun when he could outdraw them all – big and small. They said he was as fast as Old Mother Murphy's cat, which had the name of Talon. The story was that the cat escaped from lightning when it was about to strike a tree. They said that the cat saw the lightning coming – and made good its escape. The fact that no one knew Mother Murphy or her cat made no difference.

'And after the cat, there came the man,' he beamed with pride.

'And after the man, there came the boy.'

He was still bathing in his own self-glory when the policeman's words seeped through and hit his brain.

He really reeled that time. Did they call the boy Talon too?

'Stand up and face your own son, man. The son you started on a raping spree and left your mark on. I've lived under that name Talon for too long just because of you. People kept their

138

children away from me, because they believed I would grow up and turn out just like you. This was the only way I could prove myself to them, by joining the Force – to search for you.'

It all added up. Such ability. The boy had to be his son. Funny, he had no idea what the boy's mother looked like, but it did not matter any more. The boy was ready.

He suddenly realised that everything was quiet. Not even a cricket chirped. The moon was under a cloud. The old man, whose time he thought had come, had long gone to bed. His house was dark. Somewhere far away, a dog howled and he felt the fear again.

He was breathing deeply. Hope the boy did not see how nervous he was. His son. His palms were wet. He had to pull his gun. Better wipe his hands first. Unconsciously he wiped his hands on his shirt, at the side.

The flashing movement from the young policeman showed him – wiping his hands on his shirt was a mistake.

# Carlton

## Velma Pollard

'Them not in anything more than so you know. Only seh them colour turn . . .'

'Why you say that?'

'You know the father?'

'No . . .'

'Can't pass within a mile of a rum shop. Turn fool and madman same time. One day I was coming home from school. Late. And was passing the house. A hear bradang! bradang! When a look plate mash up in the road right beside my foot. Seem like him didn't leave any money with the mother and come home come find food so ask her where she get something to cook and mash up the plate dem seh is her sweetheart give her food.'

'Well every story have two side you know. You don't know what cause him to drink.'

'Mi no care. If is so them going to behave them musn't go on like seh them better than everybody.'

It wasn't long after that conversation that the niggergram had it that Carlton talking to Tootsie the biggest of the girls in that very house. In fact the story was that he used to meet her after the 27 mile-post when she was too far for anybody from school to see and walk with her to the 28 mile-post which was just before you catch her yard.

Bush have ears. That's the only way her mother could find out and ask her if Carlton talking to her. I hear that she say yes, then she say no, for while she consider herself too big to lie she didn't want her mother to start quarrel because she know that all of them feel that although Carlton so bright, brain is all him have.

Miss Marie say she really didn't have anything against Carlton himself but his family didn't come from anywhere and though it look hard to say so she didn't want any child of hers to mix up with them. 'We may be poor my dear but we come off of good table' is how she finish the discussion, I mean lecture.

Tootsie wasn't doing anything much beside walking and talking with Carlton. In fact she always say that people putting mouth on them might just make it into something none of them wasn't looking for.

Carlton was bright. Nobody could deny that. Brighter than Tootsie would ever be but he was very bitter. About the colour thing and about the class thing. And in a way he was right. In a little district where everybody was so poor why on earth should one set of poor people think themselves better than the other set? And is no point bringing in history for everybody was on the one plantation and Maasa wasn't in the habit of taking his bastard children into his house.

In any case it was hard for Carlton who used to carry cross in church and who everybody seh was so tall and handsome to have to believe them have somebody too good for him.

To tell you the truth I lost sight of both Carlton and Tootsie over time. She was taking those pupil teachers' exams you can take without going to college and he had got a place at Mico. By this time I myself was working eight–to–five at Brandt's and the sheer bother of the transportation to get home all I could do is eat and go to sleep. The weekend was to prepare my clothes for the next week, go to church Sunday and read a mystery story or two. So I wasn't too up on the gossip and everything.

Putting two and two together it seems that they had been corresponding and when he was almost ready to graduate it seems he sent a letter to her mother because by that time the drunken father had passed away. Sent to say he would like to marry Tootsie.

Those days they would send a young Mico man as headmaster to some far place where loneliness would kill him if he didn't have a wife. So mostly they would marry first or make up their mind to run the risk of interfering with underage girls in the new district.

Since he and Tootsie had been talking for about four years and writing for three, it stands to reason that he would think about her if he was thinking marriage. In any case a headmaster and

a teacher wife was a good combination in those days for it meant they would live in whichever district and help to build it up with both of them teaching at the school. They would live in the teacher's cottage and not pay any rent and so two ends could meet.

Well apparently Miss Marie, that's Tootsie's mother, put pen to paper and tell him where to get off, and come back with the same thing about table. It was the wrong thing to do. For Carlton who had only now met West Indian History and all these facts about planter class etc. had no patience with a half illiterate woman whose daughter was too good for him because her colour turn.

All the same Jackass say the world no level and is true for same time Dearest who did love Carlton bad from long time, have it to say that if she was brown skin like Tootsie, Carlton would have asked *she* to married to him and say she glad it turn out so serve him right she say. I never hear her mention how many times she fail third year and that she would not have able to get any job as teacher. And a don't hear her mention that although she did love Carlton him never ever say him did even like her as a friend. First thing her mouth don't belong to her and her mind not good.

But nobody ever expect it to end so least of all Miss Neita, Carlton mother, for he was the eldest one and she was looking to him to help

145

her with the others. Miss Neita turn pentecostal and getting spirit every night now baptize and everything. That is how she take it hard. For she did all tell everybody how little Ettie going to live with her teacher brother and going to get scholarship to High School.

I believe Carlton smoke up some weed. Not little bit. Plenty. It easy to get round here and they say if you smoke it on empty stomach people look like lizard and you can just chop them up.

The way the thing do a don't think him can even plea for manslaughter charge for it look like murder aforethought.

I couldn't go and look at it. I would never live it out. But who go, talk and tell me that Carlton build a small table right next to the path at the loneliest part of the track she usually use as short cut from the market. The cutlass must have been very sharp for they say is only a piece of skin at her neckback prevent the head from sever from the body. Of course them might all add on to the story. For I can't even understand how him get her head down on the table though people say is from the back him grab her and must be stuff her mouth so she couldn't scream. It stuff with a kerchief when they find her.

Is a child going home through the short-cut recognize Miss Marie clothes and her headtie and run screaming up the yard to Tootsie dem.

That time Carlton reach police station already

146

and show the police the blood-up cutlass and say him come to turn himself in.

I hear that Tootsie never stop bawl till she run off her head. She gone to madhouse now. And they going to hang Carlton sure as day follows night. What a foolishness though eeh. What a waste. And we lose two teacher one time.

# Heart man

## Millis D. Nicholls

Ting ling. The large bell on the Headmaster's desk gave a surprisingly small ring. Thaddeus jumped to his feet, rolled his dog-eared exercise book into a scroll and jammed it into the hip pocket of his khaki pants. Mr Best, his class master, watched him silently. His pudgy fingers were resting on the thin tamarind cane.

As Thaddeus moved away from the desk, Mr Best roared, 'Take your seat, Codrington!'

'Sir, I have to take lunch to my father too.' Thaddeus braved the piercing eye to explain. His small stomach quivered nervously.

Year after year he had watched with envy as the older boys left for lunch at eleven o'clock, instead of noon, because they had to take lunch to the cane fields. Now this year he was to have the honour of leaving early. It had been his brother's job before he had gained a scholarship to a secondary school in town. The whole thing had been explained to the master.

'Immediately, Codrington!' Mr Best thundered. Thaddeus jumped. It still impressed him that such a loud bellow could come from such an innocent-looking man. Mr Best was short and plump with a protruding stomach perched above two small

148

legs. His round cherubic face always bore a film of perspiration. Resting on his shoulders was a long head, its smooth greasy pate like freshly polished mahogany.

The trembling boy sat down. For a moment longer Mr Best regarded him. Thaddeus could not meet the bulging eyes that glowered at him from behind horn-rimmed glasses. Instead he fixed his eyes on the puff of white hair above the ears.

At the open door, two classes from Thaddeus, his friends were furiously beckoning to him. He watched them in dismay. Then one daring boy shouted, 'You can't come?'

Thaddeus dared to acknowledge the question. He shook his head. At the sound of the boy's voice, Mr Best had risen to his feet. With ease he swung his large belly around the desk and in a few strides was at the door.

'Boys!' was all they waited for before scampering for their lives down the hill.

Thaddeus held his head down to prevent his tears being seen. He had heard all about the fun the boys had on their long, hot trek to the cane fields and had eagerly looked forward to it. It never crossed his mind he'd have to take that long hot walk by himself between those lonely fields of canes in which anything could hide. The thought of it made his blood run cold.

For an hour Thaddeus glanced at the clock and fidgeted. Sometimes he wondered how far his friends had gone and when at last the bell was loudly rung to announce noon, he knew they'd be on the way back. And before the bell had stopped vibrating, he was up and running down the hill as fast as his unshod feet would go.

At the bottom his mother was impatiently waiting, the white enamel food-carrier in her hand.

'What kept you, Thad?' she asked anxiously. 'Those other boys came out long ago.' But to his relief she did not wait for an answer. She gave him a gentle push off and watched him as he gathered speed.

Before entering the village, Thaddeus armed himself with stones against the pesky dogs which usually had an obsession with his ankles. But with the village safely behind him, he looked back sadly. After all, dogs were dogs but the thing in the canes .... His small ten-year-old heart beat wildly.

The sun was scorching and heat waves rose from the road. The soft tar was forming small bubbles and even to Thaddeus's thick-soled feet it was too hot.

Soon he turned from the main road onto a narrow, rutted, dirt track that ran between a field of tall canes and a sweet potato field. The village looked far away. If something should come out of the canes and he shouted, no one would hear.

He remembered with terror hearing his mother

talk about the bodies of two young boys found lying in a cave. Their hearts had been cut out. It was supposed to have been done by the 'heart man' who lurked in the canes and caught unsuspecting little children.

Thaddeus cast a covert glance over his shoulder and quickened his steps. His small imagination was working overtime. He saw his body, minus the heart, being found by cane-cutters and his weeping mother and shocked disbelieving father identifying it. He knew the stir his death would cause in the village. And at school! They'd never cease talking about it. He saw the church, its hallowed yard thronged with curious villagers. And in the packed church his school friends singing 'Abide with Me'. They would break down and cry and have to be carried out like his mother. Yes, there she was, being supported by his father's able arms.

His reverie was rudely shattered by a rattling cough. He glanced behind and his heart stood still. All of his friends had related how, at one time or another, they had come within a hair's breadth of being caught by the 'heart man' but he had dismissed this as the outpourings of imagination. In fact, he had had many such scrapes to relate himself. But the man behind him was not imaginary.

He was old and wizened with white hair hanging in greasy strings over his bent shoulders and mingling with his bushy white eyebrows and long white beard. When he spat, Thaddeus noticed that the puckered mouth was entirely devoid of teeth. And in the eyes that should have been faded and rheumy, there was a diabolical gleam.

Thaddeus stopped walking and watched him approach. The food-carrier dangled from fingers gone suddenly nerveless.

'Hello, son,' the aged man said. 'Taking your father's food, I see.'

Thaddeus tried to answer but his trembling lips refused to form the words.

'I'm just going to the woods to get some cerosee bush for this terrible cold. Come, we can walk together.'

Thaddeus did not move. His shaking knees would not obey him. He could only turn piteous eyes on the man and await his fate.

At this the white-haired man grew angry and walked off muttering, 'Young people don't have no manners. When I was a child . . .' The words died away as the space between them widened.

At a safe distance behind, Thaddeus started walking again. When the frightening figure disappeared he gave a sigh of relief.

Further on he met his friends on their return journey. They were talking and laughing, chasing each other and rolling around on the grass. Some were sucking pieces of sugar cane, the sweet juice running unheeded down the front of their khaki shirts.

On seeing Thaddeus, they sobered up. 'Thad, you know what we saw just now? The "heart man"!' said one boy in a quaking voice. They watched him closely to see what effect that had on him.

'"Heart man", what!' Thaddeus said bravely. 'You mean that little old man with white hair and white beard? He talked to me.'

They glanced at each other. 'What did he say?'

'That he was going to the woods for cerosee bush for his cold,' was Thaddeus's reply.

'And Thad,' a sad voice said. 'You have to pass through the woods.'

At those words everyone started talking at once. They offered sympathy and one even offered to deliver a last message to his mother.

Thaddeus moved off uncertainly. Trying to hide his fear from the boys, he walked a little faster. When he glanced back, they were still there standing in a group and watching him. Soon a bend in the track hid them from him.

On either side were fields of tall, ripe sugar cane. And each time the wind passed through it Thaddeus's heart missed a beat. He glanced over his shoulders so often that he began to make himself giddy.

In front of him was the wood. But it was not the same friendly place where he had played while his father cut grass for the cows. Now it seemed mysterious and threatening. The towering casuarinas and thick-bodied mahogany with their cracked peeling bark were no longer just trees. And beneath them the dappled sunlight that danced on the grass added to the mystery. From the tree-tops monkeys peered down at him and started up a chorus of chattering which was picked up and passed on until the whole wood seemed to be laughing at him. Even the birds had lost their innocence.

Thaddeus looked back. He looked around and up and he trembled. It flashed through his mind that the old man might have changed himself into anything – a monkey perhaps or even into that dove that was watching him so closely. The terrified Thaddeus forced himself to continue walking.

'Hey, you!' He gave a cry and whirled round. Behind him, thin arms akimbo, stood the white-haired old man. The man started to move in his direction.

In one slick movement Thaddeus was off through the wood. He could not keep to the track. His feet – entirely out of control – flew over bushes and vines, dead stumps and fallen trees. He shot out of the wood gasping and panting for breath. A quick glance behind showed he was not being followed. With his heart thudding in his heaving chest, Thaddeus continued on his way.

What a narrow escape, he kept thinking. And, should he reach safety, how he'd dwell on his ability to outsmart the 'heart man'. He passed the rest of the journey either terrifying himself with thoughts of his return or calming himself with the knowledge that he could fend for himself.

At last he saw the field where his father was working. Mr Codrington watched impatiently as his son hurried up. Hungrily he snatched the food and sat under a clump of uncut canes. Before Thaddeus's famished eyes the round ball of cou-cou and fried flying fish started to disappear.

After his father had satisfied his hunger, he suddenly asked, 'You eat anything yet, boy?' Thaddeus shook his head. Mr Codrington fished in his pocket and sent his son over to the bread-cart for two glasses of mauby. He handed the food to Thaddeus and downed his drink in one long draught.

Thaddeus sat on the ground, the food-carrier between his knees, and ate. When he was through, he wiped his mouth with the back of his hand and sighed with satisfaction. Finally he related all that had passed. But, to his surprise, his father laughed.

The old man was none other than the harmless shoemaker, known and respected by everyone. The boys found in the cave? No, no, he had the story all wrong. Someone had stolen two rams, taken them to the cave where they had been slaughtered and the entrails left behind. No, there was no such thing as a 'heart man', his father assured him. It was a happy and relieved Thaddeus who started for home again.

He ran most of the way back, for with his fears of the 'heart man' banished, he began to remember Mr Best's long, thin tamarind cane. He stopped at the village standpipe and washed his hot face and feet. Under the tamarind tree his mother took the empty food-carrier, inquired if he had eaten and sent him on.

When he entered the school a hush fell. No one expected him back alive, but now he was there, they expected Mr Best to kill him. Half an hour late! It was unheard of! They eyed the cane. Thaddeus walked hesitantly up to the master.

'Sorry I am late, sir,' he muttered.

For a moment Mr Best glared. Then, 'Have you eaten?'

'Yes, sir.'

'Well, let this be a warning to you. I expect no more smart-aleck answers from you, understand?'

'Yes, sir,' Thaddeus said meekly.

'Sure you have eaten?'

'Yes, sir.'

As Thaddeus slid into his seat, he could not resist throwing a quick, triumphant glance at his friends.

# The owl and the poodledog

## Judy Stone

The satchel on Darryll's shoulder was getting lighter as he ran. So was the dawn sky.

Whap! went a rolled-up newspaper as it landed on Mr Forde's front gallery. Mr Forde's front gallery dog barked dutifully, then laid its head back down to sleep again.

Darryll ran on up Eversden Avenue. Without looking at the satchel, he was feeling in it for another paper. By the time he reached the next house, the paper was in his hand, neatly rolled and ready to throw. He hardly broke stride as he lobbed it over the gate, and he didn't wait to see it land. The crisp rolled *Guardian* flew like a stone.

Whap! Darryll heard behind him as the paper hit the step of Mrs Bryant's porch. He ran on.

Whap! to the Soogrim family.

Whap! to Miss Christian.

Whap! to the Pouchets.

Whap! to Dr Achong.

Most of the houses on Darryll's route had dogs. The Soogrims kept their hunting dog chained at night, and Miss Christian's sausage dog slept locked in the house. But Dr Achong's three fierce Dobermanns ran free in the garden.

Every morning they would be ganged up at the corner, snarling and quivering with excitement as Darryll approached. Then while he was passing they would race up and down the length of the fence against him, barking in their high hoarse voices, crouching and leaping so high he was sometimes afraid that one might actually get over the chickenwire and bite him. But he pretended to take no notice of the commotion, and kept on running.

'Dogs,' the Delivery Depot Man had warned when he first hired Darryll, 'Dogs is the onliest serious problem for the perambulating paperboy.'

The Delivery Depot Man, a fat tired person with a drooping eye, had divided the paperboys into two categories, which he liked to call 'perambulating' and 'vehicular'. The vehicular paperboys were those lucky enough to have their own bicycles. They travelled the longer routes in the area. The perambulating paperboys, such as Darryll, depended on their own feet to travel the hillside routes, which were shorter, with fewer deliveries, and so less well paid. They were harder work, too. Darryll slowed to a jogtrot as the road sloped up more steeply.

Whap! to the Andersons.

The sky was bright now, the sun edging into sight over the hills. The road was still wet from a night shower, and wisps of steam began to curl up from the warming tarmac. The air smelt of damp earth and green things.

At the next house Mrs Williams was by the gate, putting out the rubbish bin for collection. Darryll stopped and handed her the paper. She smiled automatically, without looking at him.

'Thank you, dear.'

Mrs Williams didn't know his name. None of his subscribers did. He knew all of their names though, and they'd have been surprised at how much else he knew about them. He'd even learned a lot about their characters just by the way they behaved each month-end, when he called to collect the paper money.

It was often 'Come back next week, son,' at the rich houses, while at most of the poorer houses the dollars had been carefully put aside each week ready for his call. It was apartment subscribers who gave him most trouble though; they were hardly ever at home when he called. He turned into a block now, and stuffed papers into the separate post boxes ranged on the wall. Patel. McRae. Hackett. Cherrie. Young Lai. Questel.

Back out on the road again, and up the last steep stretch to the Spanish mansion at the top.

Whap! to Judge Maharaj.

As he began to jog his way back down Eversden Avenue, Darryll could see the whole valley stretched out below him, the streets and the houses amongst the trees, with the tall buildings of the city proper in the distance, and beyond that the harbour, where a queue of cargo ships waited for a berth in the busy docks.

Darryll found himself humming a nonsense song that often drifted into his head when he saw the sea.

'The owl and the pussycat went to sea
In a beautiful pea-green boat . . .'

The song came off an old old record his mother had been given for the little ones, at one of the houses where she did domestic. People in those houses were always giving her things they didn't want any more. Some of his family's greatest treasures had appeared that way. Like the Polaroid camera. They couldn't afford to buy film, but still his mother said the camera gave the front room real class, where it sat on a doily on the cabinet.

Whap! to Mrs Guayadeen.

Darryll was working the other side of the Avenue on his way down. It was one of the richer roads on his route, but even so not everyone there took the *Guardian*. Mr Benedict didn't, for instance. Mr Benedict lived in the house Darryll was passing now. It looked neglected. Inside the broken picket fence the bush had grown so high Darryll could hardly see the house itself. White-haired Mr Benedict was almost a hermit, but Darryll knew him by sight. It wasn't so many years since Darryll himself had run with other children behind the ugly, bent old man, bawling 'Bosey-back!' and 'Cokey-eye!', and even pelting sticks. Now Darryll, the responsible wage-earner, was ashamed to remember the cruel tricks of his boy-days, and he hurried on down the hill. Whap! Whap! Whap!

He reached the end of the Avenue. The morning traffic on the main road was already busy, and he had to wait before he could cross over into Downham Crescent. There were more people about now, putting out their rubbish, backing their cars out of driveways, waving their children off to school. Stray pothounds were already nosing at the fresh rubbish.

Whap! to the Alkins family.

Only a dozen deliveries to go, and then Darryll would have to be making for school himself.

Whap! to the Dials.

Whap! to the Tuitts.

Whap-splat! to Miss de la Grenade.

Splat?

Darryll turned back and looked through the iron gate. The crisp new *Guardian* lay fast turning limp and grey where it had fallen from the gallery steps into a rainpuddle. Darryll sighed. Miss de la Grenade was a fussy spinster who lived on her own and had nothing better to do than phone up and complain about paperboys. She couldn't understand that it wasn't Darryll's fault when the press ran late, and the papers reached the Delivery Depot after he'd gone to school, and couldn't be delivered till the afternoon. The Delivery Depot Man understood that of course, but he might not be so understanding if Darryll gave Miss de la Grenade genuine cause for complaint. It would be sense to give her a fresh paper, and to pass the wet one on to a less troublesome customer.

Darryll peered up at the house, but he couldn't see anyone watching. He knew Miss de la Grenade didn't keep a dog. Softly, softly, he opened the gate and left it ajar while he tiptoed up the path. He picked up the paper and shook off the worst of the water. He was still standing beside the steps, reaching up to pass a dry *Guardian* through the gallery railing, when the front door opened. Darryll started guiltily, and then stared as what looked like a coal-black soucouyant floated down the steps past him, over the path and out of the open gate.

'Coffee!' exclaimed a young voice with a strange accent. Darryll looked up and saw standing in the doorway a skinny girl about his own age. She was looking open-mouthed, not at him, but at the open gate.

'Coffee!' she cried again.

Darryll wondered if wherever she came from this was the polite greeting.

'Er, tea!' he offered.

The girl turned and saw him for the first time.

'It was you left the stupid gate open?' she asked crossly. 'Come, for that you have to help me catch him.'

'Catch who?' asked Darryll as the girl jumped down the steps, caught his arm in a fierce grip, and hustled him along the path. She was stronger than she looked.

'I still have papers to deliver,' he protested. 'And then I have to get to school.'

'You shouldn't have let Coffee out then,' she said. 'We have to catch him quickly or he might get run over. He doesn't know his way around here yet.'

'What Coffee you talking about?'

'My poodledog, of course. There he is!' As they turned out of the gate the girl squeezed Darryll's arm painfully, and pointed. Disappearing briskly round the curve of the Crescent was the coal-black soucouyant.

'Poodledog? It look more like a perambulating Afro to me,' said Darryll sourly, pulling his arm free. 'Why you call it Coffee?'

'Not Coffee, Cuffie, you stupidee,' said the girl, again tugging Darryll with her as she began to run. 'Come on, hurry, he's going towards the main road.'

'Why you call him Cuffie, then?' Darryll asked as they ran. He tried to ignore the satchel bouncing the undelivered papers on his hip with every step.

'You don't know Cuffie?' The girl was surprised. 'Cuffy's the first black hero of Guyana. He led the revolution.'

'That where you come from, Guyana?'

'Of course. But my dad decide to take a job here. We smuggled Cuffie through in a basket.

164

We only staying with my auntie while we find a place to live. I'm Joan, you know.'

'Well, my name Darryll, and it look like your Cuffie start he own revolution, from the rear.' Darryll was grinning for the first time since he'd met this bossy girl. A shrill barking had broken out ahead of them, and they rounded the curve to see the small black dog chasing a yellow cat across the Crescent. On the far side the cat hesitated at a high wire fence, then doubled round and came flying straight towards Darryll and Joan, with Cuffie in full cry behind. At the last minute the cat saw the two and swerved back towards the main road. Cuffie couldn't change direction fast enough. He came pelting between Darryll's legs with such force that the next thing the boy knew he was knocked flat on the pavement.

'Cuffie! Catch him, catch him!' Joan shrieked, grabbing wildly. They both missed. Still yapping, Cuffie was off again after the cat.

'Idiot! What kind of boy you are, you can't even hold a poodledog,' said Joan in disgust as Darryll picked himself up. She didn't wait for a reply, but went running after her dog.

'What kind of girl you are, bigmouth!' said Darryll, knowing she couldn't hear him. But now he found he was personally vexed with this poodledog, and meant to see it caught. He began to run, pausing just long enough to hang his satchel on the first gate he passed.

He reached the main road at the moment when

the yellow cat dived under a passing car. Cuffie followed close behind, disappearing between the wheels. Joan screamed in fright and Darryll was only just in time to pull her back. There were squeals of brakes from two taxis travelling one way, and from the enormous red rubbish-truck rumbling past the other.

'You looking to die, girl?' called one of the men riding on the truck.

Joan didn't answer. She looked sick and trembling. Cuffie's yapping had stopped abruptly. But when the traffic cleared there was no sign of the dog, not even the crushed body that Darryll had half expected.

All at once they heard Cuffie's voice again, somewhere across the road, out of sight. Joan gasped.

'Eversden Avenue,' said Darryll. 'Come on.' He pulled her safely over the road and round the corner. Far up the Avenue they saw little Cuffie with his back to a dustbin, barking bravely. The yellow cat had vanished. A ring of dogs was closing in on Cuffie. Large, snarling, gaunt, hungry pothounds.

'Cuffie!' Joan cried. At the same moment the biggest dog pounced. With a squeal of terror Cuffie scuttled between its legs and away up the hill, with the pack baying behind him.

'They'll murder him!' Joan cried helplessly. Darryll ran up the Avenue as he'd never run before, panting, heart pounding, sweat in his eyes.

166

He saw Cuffie slip through a narrow gap in a broken fence, and for a moment thought the little dog was safe, till the pack leader found a bigger hole and led his mob through. Darryll scrambled through the same hole, with Joan behind him, and pushed through the bush inside. He couldn't see what was happening ahead of him when the excited baying suddenly turned to frightened yelps, and a moment later the pothounds were racing back past him, fighting to escape through the fence. There was a sound of rain, and Darryll was suddenly soaked to the skin. He struggled out of the bush onto a small, neat lawn, and there stood old Mr Benedict, with a dripping garden hose in his hand, a frown on his face, and a small black dog taking sanctuary at his feet.

'Cuffie!' Joan pushed past Darryll to pick up her runaway. 'You all right, you wickedness.' She hugged Cuffie, and he licked her cheek.

'Hold him,' she ordered Darryll in her old bossy manner, and before he knew what she was doing she had thrust the dog into his hands and flung her arms round bosey-back Mr Benedict to give him a fierce hug.

'Thank you for saving Cuffie,' she said.

Mr Benedict's cokey eye twinkled.

'Well, my dear, it didn't seem right for so many to gang up on one little pothound,' he said.

'Cuffie's a poodledog,' said Darryll.

Joan looked embarrassed.

'Well, he's not really, he just looks a bit like one.'

'And maybe he acts a bit like one,' said Mr
Benedict, nodding his head, 'and that's what
annoyed the pack. If he'd just behaved like the
pothound he is, they'd have left him alone.'

Darryll looked at the subdued, wet ball of fur in
his hands. He didn't really know what a true true
poodledog should look like, but, if it looked like
a perambulating Afro, right now Cuffie looked
more like an advertisement for pomade.

'You'd better come inside and get dry,' said Mr
Benedict. They followed him onto his gallery and
he brought them each a towel. He also brought a
cardboard box.

'Look inside,' he said. The box was empty
except for one fluffy brown lump the size of an
orange, pressed into a corner. The lump didn't
seem to have a head, but it was breathing.

'Ugh, it's a rat,' said Joan.

'No, it's a bird,' said Darryll.

'It's a jumbie bird,' said Mr Benedict. 'A pygmy
owl. Sometimes they forget they're night birds and
try to fly by day, and then all the other birds mob
them and try to kill them, even the hummingbirds.'

'No!' Joan was shocked.

'I had to rescue this one yesterday,' Mr Benedict
went on. 'You see, it's not only dogs need to keep
in mind who they are. And it's not only dogs have
to learn to live and let live. It even happens with
people too, eh, Darryll?'

Darryll felt his face burn. The old man had
recognised him from those boy days.

'How you know my name?' he asked, amazed.

'Oh, I may not take a newspaper,' said Mr Benedict, smiling, 'but I know what goes on under my nose.'

And he winked a kindly cokey eye.

# Anancy and Mongoose

## Velma Pollard

(a modern Anancy Story)

Long long ago when all the people who are big now, were little, Mongoose lived in the bush and Anancy lived in the ceiling. You don't know but at that time, whenever you looked up in the house you would see rectangular pieces of wood called shingles. And between the shingles and along the V-shaped corners they call eaves you would see Anancy's web; and inside the web you would see Anancy. A little farther on you would see Mrs. Anancy, with a soft white pouch under her belly, with all the little Anancys in it.

But plaster came in and celotex came in and when you look up in your house now you see squares of plaster or squares of celotex. And zinc came in, so some people look up now and see sheets of zinc. And there was nowhere for Anancy to live.

As usual, Anancy had a bright idea. He went to Brother Mongoose who had a nice house in the bush and greeted him:

'Breda Mon . . . Goosy.'

'Hey Breda Nansi dis lang time mi no see you. Wa happm?'

'Mi wohzhn't here you know Breda Mon. Mi wozh in America. One of the chilvren sen fa mi. In fak a hit mek mi come here now. Mi see something over there mi have to tell you bout. Whole heap a man de a Merica like you, you know. But dem no live a bush. Dem live a town. Big tall white man all have dem jus a hol aan pan dem han, pan dem shoulder, pan dem ches an a feed dem wid some nut dem call ches-nut. So mi a seh paraps you shoulda go de, or even go a town mek big man put you fi live iina dem house an hol aan pan dem han.'

'A we yaa seh Breda Nansi . . . fi true?'

'You tink mi woulda fool you Breda Mon? Look how long mi an you know one aneda! Ef you mek up you mine mi no wi help you pack so go lidong a Constant Spring golf course we nuff white man de.'

'You know Breda Nansi mi mighta try see.'

So Mongoose went in and called Mrs. Mongoose and the children and explained that they were about to go to find a better life. They were about, as they say in books, to relocate. Anancy helped them pack and led them to the golf course. There he left them to seek their fortune.

Meanwhile Anancy collected all the things he had left with various friends when shingle roofs got hard to find and moved with his wife into Mongoose's spacious house in the bush.

Day passed and night came. Night went and morning came and Mr. Mongoose and his family lay with their luggage on the golf course. A few Americans came and looked at them and said 'Gee whizz they look like squirrels. Tails a little short and hair not enough but . . . my my my.' And they walked past.

Mongoose ran across the street from time to time to see if anything better was on the other side but each time he would come back and tell the sad-faced Mrs. Mongoose and the hungry children there was nothing. At first he wouldn't let her, and he wouldn't let the children, cross the street, and whenever he did, he would look carefully first up street then down street before he went. Half-way across he would stop, look quickly both ways again, then cross. Sometimes the traffic was very thick and Mongoose thought the stream of cars would never end.

Meanwhile Brother Anancy and Mrs. Anancy relaxed deep down in the cool of Mongoose's house. Nobody could see them because the house is underground. At night Anancy himself would go out and steal food to store. He and Mrs. Anancy lived a happy, retired life.

Now early every morning, before cars come out, Mongoose crosses the street. Nowadays he sends Mrs. Mongoose, and sometimes, every now and then, one of the bigger children. And he hopes one day he will see Anancy. He can't go home. Neither he himself nor his wife nor any of the children had paid attention when they followed Anancy to the golf course. They have no idea what

174

route they came. Now upstreet and downstreet look the same. There are no plants to smell, no mud tracks to notice. And they don't understand the city. Chewing gum and cigarette butts are hard to eat and the children look very thin. Mrs. Mongoose tries not to say much. She doesn't want to blame Brother Mon. But she misses her home and the kitchen garden on the land above it.

And now the tall white men with metal sticks in their hands, don't even look at them anymore.

So when you drive or walk near the golf course road and you see mongoose crossing and re-crossing the street and looking sharply from side to side . . . is Anancy cause it.

. . . Jackmandoora mi no choose none.

# The paddy-man

## David King

Every Saturday morning, for as long, almost, as I can remember, a squat barrel-chested little man passed our way, pushing a handcart up the street and bringing a few gaunt old hens out of the yards on both sides of the road.

At first my acquaintance with him was confined to a rather absent-minded observation of his activities from our upstairs window at the front of the house. Really I should have been busy with my homework for school on Monday. I seldom in those days got much opportunity to play games. In the first place, we were new in the neighbourhood, and my mother did not approve of any of our neighbours, and so would let us have nothing whatsoever to do with them. Secondly, the Headmaster of my school had told my mother that if I studied hard, I might win a scholarship to secondary school like my bigger brother.

'Get you paddy. Come, the paddy-man passing. Paddeeeeey!'

His high-pitched voice cut its way through the babble of women's voices next door as they spread their clothes on the grass for the sun to bleach them. No ship was in port today and so the men

176

were playing dominoes in the cake shop opposite. Soon the paddy-man came into view. He went toiling past our front gate and heaved to a stop, almost deferentially polite – so it always seemed to me – a few yards beyond. He pulled a large brown handkerchief from a hip pocket, wiped his face and each one of his fingers. He walked round his cart, tugging at the bags and opening them out at the necks. Then with a final shout:

'Come quick!' he disappeared into the shop opposite for a few moments' rest in the shade.

He was an Indian – handsome, middle-aged, with long, thick, jet-black hair under a rather shapeless felt hat. His khaki shirt was always unbuttoned right up to his round hairy stomach. He wore no shoes at first but in later years he got himself a cheap pair of yachtin' shoes.

His cart was soon surrounded by the women from the tenement next door, some with old iron pots on their hips.

'Come quick, man. You think we able to stand up heh for wait 'pon you all day? Come, man, come.'

The paddy-man gave his face a final wipe with his shirt sleeve and approached the cart.

'How much you dirty paddy selling for today?'

'Put four pint in heh, and don't bother gi' me any trash!'

The paddy-man filled the pots under the hard watchful eyes of the women. Most of them were negro. They cracked jokes and belly-laughed

177

among themselves, their eyes never leaving the tin-cup measure of the paddy-man, but trying, it appeared, to make friends with the man, to draw him into them so that they could get an extra half-pint or maybe so that he might lose count of who had paid him what, or something. The paddy-man made cautious replies and measured the paddy out carefully. He never smiled. When they asked for 'truss' he shook his head sadly but firmly. Sometimes he would give in, however, and enter the amount owed in a dirty little notebook. Sometimes to avoid any argument over the amount owed he would go with them into the yard and write up the debt, a stroke for each pint, on a post or on the unpainted wall. The following week he insisted that they pay up before they got their paddy. Somehow they found the money.

At first, half-joking, they began to talk of 'that stingy coolie dog' as his cart appeared in the street. But times got hard and the price of paddy went up in the market they began to call him simply 'dat coolie'. They began to hate him.

One day a quarrel broke out at the paddy-cart. A stout loud-mouthed woman named Miss Bertha accused the paddy-man of measuring the paddy short. She called the whole yard to witness how this damn thief was scooping out her paddy with his finger from the top of the measure. She kept saying over and over 'This story not going to end here.'

Miss Bertha had seven children. Her 'husband' was a sailor. He was a big man with long rope-like muscles in his back. The paddy-man flung an extra half-pint into Miss Bertha's pot before he wheeled his cart up the street. He said nothing but he was muttering to himself in Hindi as he pushed his cart away, and, in the distance he looked like a tiny tormented figure about to be overwhelmed by a very heavy burden.

All that afternoon the women quarrelled in the yard, everybody now convinced that their suspicions of the paddy-man had been long-standing and just. Miss Bertha maintained an injured silence far more damning than words. The rancour had now spread to the others. Miss Rose the washerwoman was spreading sheets and white shirts on the grass behind her house with sharp angry jerks of her body.

'What I really want to know,' she was saying to Miss Linda, 'is where he get that tin-cup he using with the paddy. Is dat I want to know. I did tell all you from long that the coolie digging out we eye with he thiefing ways.'

Miss Linda called God to judge her if the brute did not mix stones and dirt with the paddy and sell it. She came out on to her landing. She was a young woman, brown-skinned with firm flesh and skin as smooth as a baby's. Her hair was in curlers and she was wearing a man's shirt several sizes too big for her.

'Watch me if you think is lie.' She held her

well-shaped arms high above her head, then opened her palms wide. A tiny cloud of grey dust appeared suspended in the air as if by magic and spread downwards to the ground. A few straying fowls darted to the spot beneath the steps and pecked about uncertainly in the mud and grass beneath.

I had become so engrossed in what was going on next door that I did not hear my mother calling me. I hastily dropped the book I should have been reading and went into the kitchen. She gave me money and a list of things to buy for her in the market. Our neighbours' quarrelling irritated my mother. At first she had been able to ignore the loud laughter and squabbling from next door. But things had gone hard for us for some time. The burden of keeping my brother and myself in school since my poor father's death was slowly beginning to tell on her. The poorer we got, the more our neighbours' brawls seemed to affect her.

One night that very week, after dinner, we were sitting round the dining table hard at work when there was a loud crash from next door followed by the tinkle of broken glass upon stone. We looked at each other blankly. There was a momentary hush; then the sound of a woman's voice from next door.

'George,' the voice said quietly but firmly, as if speaking to a stubborn child, 'come out of the woman's house.'

There was another loud crash and the distinct bump of something hard bouncing on a wooden floor. For a dreadful moment I thought it was the paddy-man come back to avenge his outraged dignity, but now with growing curiosity I drew the window blind just a little to one side and peeped out.

The moon was shimmering gently on the fronds of the coconut tree and on the zinc roofs clustered in the yard. Dark human shapes were emerging on the landings of the houses all around. An empty tin rattled as a foot brushed against it in the darkness. A woman was standing one arm akimbo in front of one of the houses in the yard. It was the only house in the yard with glass windows and a lamp was burning dimly somewhere inside. The woman's arm swung. There was another loud crash. Her voice spoke again.

'George, like you don't hear – I say to come out of the woman house?'

The only response from the house was that the light went out. Excited whispering broke out all around and people began to gather in the street. Someone giggled and the children began to jump about and clap their hands. My mother put on her hat, went down the road and came back with the police.

Next Saturday, when the paddy-man appeared, his cart was more heavily laden than usual.

'Come get you paddy and corn!'

He brought the cart to a jolting stop, walked

181

around the cart and went perspiring heavily to buy a soft drink. I noticed that one of the wheels of the cart had begun to wear a deep rut in the dirt at the roadside. Everybody went to the cart. Miss Bertha, did not appear.

'Miss Bertha,' the paddy-man called out, 'I got new paddy today. Look how it fresh and nice. Come bring you pan quick. It will soon done.'

Miss Bertha appeared on the landing.

'How the paddy stay?' She shot the question at Miss Linda.

'The paddy good today Miss B. Eh eh!. . . is a wonder.'

The paddy-man opened the mouth of a large crocus bag a little wider.

'Is what we have hiding in the bag?' Miss Bertha asked.

'Some plantain and eddoe and a lil'l sweet potato,' the paddy-man said before Miss Linda could speak. 'How much you want?'

There had been a shortage of ground provisions all week. The women carefully examined the plantains and some talk passed between them in low tones. The price was high, but they would buy. A happy atmosphere of friendly bickering surrounded the cart.

My mother called me, put some money in my hand and to my surprise told me to go and buy some plantains from the cart. I went down the steps and through the gate. As I approached the cart, the haggling stopped and I felt the eyes of the neighbours on me. The paddy-man turned to me immediately.

'Yes, massa, what for you today?'

What for me today .... He was treating me like an old customer. I felt bigger. 'How much for the plantains?'

'Yes, massa, nice green plantain. How much you want?'

I had spoken a little too quickly because I was nervous. He had only caught the last word. The women moved impatiently. I felt as if I was acting in some strange play, and that I had forgotten the lines I had learnt.

'What a pound for the plantain?' My voice to my surprise sounded loud and hard. The paddy-man understood me now. I realised with a shock that that was how the women talked to him.

'Eight cents a pound. How much you want? Four pound?'

'Two pound. I want two pounds.'

He selected the better-looking plantains for me from among the worm-eaten ones. His brown hairy hands were streaming with sweat, the long hairs sticking flat against the skin. He smelt sharply of sweat and paddy dust. As he counted the change slowly into my hand, his eyes passed over my face. He had curious eyes, light-coloured and haggard-looking. I retreated with the plantains and my change into my yard. As I closed the gate firmly behind me, a sudden warm feeling went out from me to the paddy-man. I remembered the roughness in my voice when I was at the cart and deep inside me I felt ashamed. I never went to the paddy-cart again.

The months passed by. As exam-time approached, I developed the habit of spending my Saturday mornings at the public library and I saw little of the paddy-man for some time. At Christmas my mother gave little gifts to many of the children from next door. They came up the back steps and accepted their little parcels, each carefully wrapped in Christmas paper. A few said: 'Thanks'. Others turned and went down the back steps without a word. Their mother swept down their own steps, treader by treader, pretending not to look. After that they began to stare at us over the fence even more curiously than before. Miss Linda said something to the others that sounded like '. . . playing white', before going inside.

The paddy-man had by now got himself a pair of cheap canvas shoes, but apart from this there was little or no change in his appearance or behaviour. For about two or three weeks, there had been a little boy helping him to push the heavy cart but soon he was alone again. He began to complain loudly about 'the modern-day pickny dem . . .', which seemed to strike some sympathetic chord in the hearts of the women at the cart. The paddy-man cursed the boy. The women too cursed the boy. After that everybody's mind came back to the paddy.

One Saturday morning, two weeks before my exam, I stayed at home reading in the front gallery overlooking the street as I used to do earlier in the year.

'Padeeeeeey! Get you paddeeeeey! Come the paddy-man passing . . .'

As usual the high pitch of the paddy-man's voice in the distance began its far but steady interference with the other noises in the street. It interrupted them and changed their pattern. Only the hard slamming of the bone dominoes went on unchanged and unhurried as before. Finally the paddy-cart arrived opposite to my gate, came to a stop and the paddy-man began to walk towards the cake shop. I glanced through the open window absentmindedly, watching the women gather round the cart. It looked at first as if everything was just as I remembered it. The faces were the same, the talk was the same, even the fowls gathering round the cart looked as if they were the same.

But there was something different somehow, something wrong that I could not put my finger on; and it worried me somehow. The paddy-man returned to the cart and began to sell. It was as if I found the whole scene more threatening somehow, more . . . . Suddenly I realised what was wrong. The paddy-man had stopped short of his usual spot. He had brought the cart to a halt directly in front of our gate and the left cart-wheel had already begun the process of creating for itself a deep, smooth-fitting rut. I began to notice also that he was glancing in the direction of our house from time to time as he measured out the paddy. Then something strange happened. When he had sold to everyone, he left his cart, opened our gate and disappeared from my view. Then after a few seconds I heard him calling up the back steps to my mother to send somebody for the paddy.

My mother's hair was now showing signs of greying. If a glass fell and broke in the house, it was enough to trigger off an angry outburst from her. She dried her fingers on the kitchen towel and took off her apron. Then she picked up the pail and went out for the paddy.

After that my mother often locked herself in her bedroom, and we would hear her singing softly the verse of a hymn, then the rustling of leaves as she turned the pages of her Bible.

A few weeks later a quarrel arose in our yard. The paddy-man's voice could be heard distinctly, wailing and complaining downstairs. I dashed down the back steps to see what was the matter. My mother was calling the paddy-man a thief. The man was standing on an old dining table counting a long line of chalk-marks which had appeared, like ancient hieroglyphics along one of the ledges overhead. The domino game in the shop opposite came to a stop. The paddy-man continued to count.

Then Miss Bertha began to quarrel.

'But what anybody call to this thing! But all you look 'pon this man! Like he getting too big for his pants or something.'

'He too damn presumptuous to walk in the lady own yard, and say – and say 'bout she thief.'

The shop-keeper, a short middle-aged black man was coming across the road. He came through the open front gate and approached my mother. He introduced himself and I saw him point in the direction of his shop. He expressed shock at the paddy-man's behaviour and asked what was it all about. My mother began to explain and he listened punctuating her words with frequent nodding and shaking of his head. Finally he put a brown envelope into my mother's hand and said something, repeating the words 'Whenever you can,' several times. My mother began to say something, but he interrupted her, nodding his head in my direction.

'So the boy soon take his exam.'

'Yes,' said my mother. They both looked at me, their backs to the paddy-man. 'The teacher says he might win a government scholarship this year.' The shop-keeper began to nod again. Then he went back to his shop.

My mother paid the paddy-man in full and asked me to see that the paddy-man rubbed off all the marks on the house and that he closed the gate behind him. Then I could go and study at the library. She turned and went back up the stairs.

The paddy-man left our yard, muttering to himself in Hindi, and began to push his cart away from the gate. A stone rattled against the boards at the side of the cart, and a woman gave the little boy standing beside her a quick slap on the arm. Then she suddenly bent double at the waist in a convulsion of dry, mirthless laughter. She turned and went inside. Dominoes slapped hard on the shop table.

Miss Rose, the washerwoman, returned to finish spreading her white sheets and shirts to sun on the long grass growing at the front of her yard. She had only one shirt left to spread. She looked around for a place to put it. Then she hung it carefully on our fence.

# Ascot

## Olive Senior

'That Ascot goin go far,' Mamma say, 'Mark my word.'

'Yes. Him goin so far him goin ennup clear a prison,' Papa say. Every time you mention Ascot name to Papa these days the big vein in Papa forehead tighten up and you know he trying hard to control himself.

'Oh gawd when all is said an done the bwoy do well Jackie. Doan go on so,' Mamma say.

'De bwoy is a livin criminal. Do well me foot. Look how him treat him family like they have leprosy. Deny dem. Is so you wan you pickney behave. Cho woman. Yu was always a fool,' and with that Papa jam him hat on him head and take off down the road.

See here! I don't think Papa ever recover from the day that Ascot come back. This Ascot is a tall red bwoy that born round here. Mamma and all the rest of the women did like Ascot who is Miss Clemmy outside son for Ascot come out with fair skin and straight nose and though him hair not so good it not so bad neither. And nobody know who Ascot father is but is not Dagoman who Miss Clemmy living with all these years for you only have to look at Dagoman to see that.

Anyhow this Ascot tall no langilalla and him not so bad looking though him have a mouth so big that when him smile him lip curl but all the women just melt when Ascot smile and say how him bound to go far.

But all that the men remember bout Ascot is that Ascot is a real ginnal and also that Ascot have the biggest foot that anybody round here ever see. Especially Papa.

One time Papa used to miss all kind of thing from the buttery. Now when Papa not looking all we children would tief in there and take like two finger ripe banana or some small thing but nothing serious. Papa would find out and accuse we and we would lie but none of we could lie so good because Mamma use to beat the lying out of we and Papa would know the culprit right away so nobody would take it serious. Papa used to say he wouldn't grudge his own children nothing, but is the principle of the thing and he don't like to have his authority undermine and that sort of thing.

Well anyway, one time a whole heap of big thing start disappear from the buttery – a brand new cutlass, some yam head, a crocus bag and finally, a big bunch of banana that Papa was ripening for the church Harvest Festival. Well sah, all we children used to run in the buttery and look at the bunch of banana till we eye water but none of us would bold enough to touch it for is the most beautiful thing that we ever see in our whole life.

So the Saturday morning before the Harvest Festival one bangarang nuh bus at the house! Papa go into the buttery and find the whole bunch of banana nuh gone way clean. Jesus. You should hear the noise he make. Then him calm down and he just stand there a look at the ground for a long time and is sad we think Papa sad for is the best bunch of banana that he ever grow. But finally him say 'All right. Is Ascot do it. See him guilt there plain as day. Is Ascot one have foot that size.' And is true for we all look at the footprint on the ground and we know is Ascot do it.

Papa say to we 'Doan say a word' and him send off to call Ascot while him close the buttery door and tell all of we to go sit on the verandah like nothing happen. So Ascot come grinning as usual like him expecting food and Papa say, 'Come Ascot me bwoy Harvest Festival pospone and we gwine nyam banana caan done tidday.'

As Papa say the word 'banana' Ascot not grinning so wide again and he say as if him deaf 'Wha Mass Jackie?' and we all start giggle for him voice come out squeaky like muss-muss and Papa say, 'Yes bwoy feas tidday.' Then we all walk round to the buttery and Papa throw the door wide open and the first thing that everybody see is the hook where the banana was hanging up empty as night.

'Oh gawd where me Harvest Festival banana gaan-o,' Papa shout out, 'Ascot look ya me banana no gaan.'

'Wha Mass Jackie,' Ascot say but you could see that him hanging back. 'Nutten could go so afta nobody bol'nuf come in ya an walk weh wid hu banana.'

Papa just stand there for a while as if him studying the situation and then him say, 'Ascot me bwoy, yu an me gwine have to play poleece an search fe clues.'

Meantime Papa there looking at the ground and then he make as if him just see the footprint and he say, 'Ascot look here my bwoy,' and by now Ascot look like shame-me-lady macca that just done step on. Papa say 'But wait Ascot. Puddon yu foot ya.'

And Ascot bawk out, 'Laaad Mass Jackie is nuh me do it sah.'

Papa say, 'No? Den puddon yu foot ya yu tiefing brute,' and make to grab after Ascot. But Ascot jump back so braps and fly off like streak lightning. And from that day on, Papa swear that him wash him hand of Ascot.

Ascot stay far from the house for a good while and anytime he see Papa him take off to bush for Papa walking bout and threatening to shoot him for him banana though you know after a time that Papa enjoying himself so much telling everybody how him frighten Ascot that you can see that him dont mind bout the banana so much after all. But Ascot really have no shame at all and little by little him start hang round the kitchen again when Papa not there and Mamma would feed him till finally him round the house almost as often as before.

Anyway my big brother Kenny did come up from May Pen one Sunday and Ascot come up to him when Papa back turn and ask if he couldn't give him job as gardener. And as Kenny don't know bout the banana – and he must be the only person Papa forget to tell – Kenny say alright. And although Papa warn Kenny that him taking up trouble Mamma say that at heart Ascot is really a decent honest boy and that all he need is opportunity so when Kenny ready to leave Ascot arrive with him bundle and seat himself off in Kenny car please no puss! 'No matter how hard yu wuk and how much money yu make yu will nevva find shoes for dem doan mek them in fe yu size,' was Papa's last word to Ascot.

Well sah, as Papa predict Ascot dont stay long with Kenny. Little after Ascot gone there we get letter from Kenny say he sending Ascot home for Ascot dont want do nothing round the yard and all he do all day is jump behind the wheel of motor car the minute people back turn, and make noise like say he driving. The letter arrive one day and the next day we get another letter say Ascot take his belonging and a few other things that didn't belong to him so maybe he on the way home and good riddance. Anyway, Ascot never turn up at all and Miss Clemmy getting ready to go out of her mind that he in trouble till she get message say Ascot in Kingston learning to drive.

And then one day bout a year after, who arrive but Ascot! He wearing a shirt and tie and pants that too short but is alright because it allow you to see Ascot shoes better. Ascot nuh get shoes! See here, he wearing the biggest pair of puss boot that ever make. It big so till everybody from miles around run to look at Ascot foot in shoes like is the eight wonder of the world. Ascot tell we he driving in Kingston though most people don't believe him. But mark you, from Ascot small he used to tell me how him life ambition was to dress up in white clothes and drive a big white car.

So Ascot stay round for a while doing not a thing and he not smiley-smiley so much and in fact Ascot get very quiet. Then one day him nuh announce that him get paper to go States as farm worker and the next day him leave us again dress up in him big brown puss boots.

Well it look like Ascot dead fe true this time for nobody hear from him till government send a man down to Miss Clemmy to find out if she hear from him for he skip the farm work in Florida and just disappear right after he reach. Poor Miss Clemmy frighten so till and crying the whole time now for Ascot for the man say that they going to prison Ascot if they find him for he does do a criminal thing. But still not a word from Ascot and everybody give him up for dead or prison except Papa who say that the cat which is the incarnation of the devil have nine life and that is Ascot. About three years pass and Miss Clemmy nuh get letter from the United States. She beg me read it to her and it say:

Dear Ma

wel I am here in New York is a big plase and they have plenty car I am going to get One

yr loving son Ascot

And he enclose one dollar and no return address.
About two years pass and then Miss Clemmie get
another letter from the USA which she beg me
read. Is from Ascot and it say:

Dear Mother,
        wel here I am in
Connecticut  Connecticut is
big plais   I driving Car
two £ year now but is not
wite
    yr loving Son Ascot

And he send two dollar. Then about a year later she get another letter that say:

Dear Mother
 Chicago is a big plais
I drivin wite ✷ car for
wite man but he don make me
 where wite is black unform
 so I mite leave
 yr loving son Ascot

And he send three dollar. 'He-he,' say Papa to Miss Clemmy, 'By de time yu get fifty letter yu nuh rich.' But Miss Clemmy don't laugh for she say she sure Ascot leading bad life. And that was the last time she get letter from Ascot.

After that so much time pass that all of we almost forget Ascot. One time Papa did get a little banana bonus so I go to town and come back with some nice meat and Papa go and dig him good yam and the day after that we cook a backra dinner. Papa just sitting on the verandah making the smell kill him and telling me and Mamma to hurry up. Next thing we know a big white car nuh draw up at the gate and turn into the yard. 'Eh-eh is who dat?' Papa say and we all run to the verandah. All we can see is the front door open and two foot stick outside.

'Jesus have mercy is Ascot,' say Mamma. 'Is Ascot one have foot big so.'

'Ascot me teet. Whe Ascot fe get big car from?' Papa say.

But lo and behold. Nuh Ascot! Ascot dress in white from head to toe and though him plenty fatter him teeth kin same way. And a woman get out of the car with him and you can see she foreign from the clothes she wearing and the colour of her hair though I swear afterward is wig.

Eh-eh, Ascot him nuh rush up to my mother and start hug and kiss her, 'Aunt Essie, Aunt Essie,' he crying.

'*Aunt* Essie,' Papa say, 'Since when she anyting but *Miss* Essie' but Ascot rushing to him acry 'Uncle Jackie' and next thing we know he hugging Papa who turn purple he so vex. 'Cousin Lily' – that's me he talking to – and he there hugging me too before I know what is happening. Papa stand there with him mouth open like him seeing rolling calf but Ascot so busy a chat he don't notice.

'An this,' he say 'is my wife Anthea' and the lady say hello in this deep American accent.

'Ascot then is really you,' Mamma saying and she look like she almost crying.

'Yes Aunt Essie is real wonderful to see you' Ascot say and his American accent so thick you could cut it with knife.

'Cousin Lily,' he say, taking my hand, 'Can I speak to you for a minute,' and he haul me off into the parlour. 'Cousin Lily, you are my friend for a long time now. Right?' So I say, 'Right.' 'Okay, so just pretend that you is my cousin and this is my house, right'. Eh-eh, I don't know what Ascot playing but this whole thing sweet me so I say okay and call Mamma and tell her. Of course she dont understand what really going on so I keep my finger cross.

By the time I get back to the verandah Ascot is there like a man that make out of nothing but energy, is not the Ascot that leave here at all. He just walking and talking and moving his hand up and down the whole time. Then he say to the wife, 'Come let me show you around my birthhouse' and next thing he leading her through the whole house as if is him own it. Mamma just stand there with her jaw drop and Papa mouth set while the vein in him forehead beating hard. Then Ascot take the wife into the yard and he there waving him hand and telling her 'And this is my property and this is my coconut tree – you ever see coconut tree with

coconut before – and this is where I does bathe when I small and this is our water tank that I did help build.'

See ya pappy-show! Well that was bad enough but next thing he gone to Papa cocoa tree and he there saying 'And this is a cocoa tree from which you does get chocolate bet you never see that before' and he grab up Papa cutlass and chop off one of the cocoa pod and start cut it up to show her the seed.

Papa start to get up but Mamma say 'Jackie!' and he just sink back down into the chair as if he defeated. Then Ascot and him wife come back on the verandah and sit down and Ascot cock up him foot on the railing. He start chatting away but Papa not opening him mouth and so Mamma and me there carrying on conversation. Ascot say him driving him own big white car and he work in a garage but he like one of the boss man now and he so happy that he had to bring his wife back to show her the birthplace where he spent his happy childhood. He also say they staying in hotel in Kingston and they going back that night and is rent they rent the car they driving. That was one thing but next thing I go ask the wife what she do and she announce that she really is a teacher but right now she just finishing up her Master Degree. Master Degree? – Ascot marry woman with Master Degree and he dont even finish third standard in school. See here Lord. We all speechless again.

So Ascot there chatting and chatting and we all getting hungrier and hungrier and the food smelling better and better and it don't look as if they out to leave so finally Mamma say in her best speaky-spoky voice 'Would you like a bite to eat' and I know is show off she showing off on Ascot wife who have Master Degree that she have good food in the house.

'Yes thank you Aunt Essie is long time since I taste yu cooking,' Ascot say and cross him leg. Papa give Mamma such a look that thank God none of them did see. Mamma never see neither she so please that she entertaining somebody with Master Degree for the highest qualified person she ever meet is Extension Officer and that dont count because is only agriculture him did learn. So we put out all the food that we did cook and Mamma take out her best crockery and send down to Miss Melda to borrow the glasses that she did just get from her daughter-in-law in the States and everybody sit down to eat – everybody except Papa who say he not hungry and he dont want anything to eat and we know better than to argue with him when he vex like that.

Well sah. Ascot put down a piece of eating there that I couldn't describe to you and when he done the table clean as a whistle. As soon as they eat done Mamma say 'Well Ascot I suppose you want to spend some time with Clemmy,' and Ascot say 'Clemmy – Oh yes' as if he just remember her and he jump up and say, 'soon be back' and drive off to see Miss Clemmy. I tell you that was the biggest piece of extraness I ever see because Miss Clemmy live in the next bend in the road and if we want to call her all we do is lean out the kitchen window and shout. But Ascot drive gone and he stay away a long time and I believe is to confuse him wife that Miss Clemmy live a long way away.

About half an hour afterward Ascot arrive with the car full with Miss Clemmy and Dagoman and all the children dress in their best clothes. Ascot say to him wife, 'And this is Clemmy and Dagoman' and Dagoman lift his hat and bow and I swear Miss Clemmy drop a curtsey.

'Oh and do you live nearby,' say the wife to Miss Clemmy.

'Yes Maam, jus roun de corner'.

'And are all these your children?'

'Yes'm Hascot is the heldes but is not de same fader.'

The wife give Ascot a look to kill and is plain she never realise that is Ascot mother.

'But I did almost grow with Aunt Essie' Ascot say quick but you could see him turning red.

'Clemmy,' my mother call her inside, 'Look her Clemmy,' she tell her, 'is you daughter-in-law that what you calling her maam for. Dont keep on saying yes maam no maam to everything she say. You hear me.'

'Yes maam,' say Miss Clemmy and while I inside clearing the table all I can hear is Miss Clemmy saying 'yes maam, no maam' to everything her daughter-in-law saying.

Miss Clemmy keep on looking at Ascot as if he is stranger and Dagoman sit on the bench outside as if he too fraid to come near the lady. The children start play around the car and make as if to open the door and Ascot snap at them so till my mother had to say 'Hi Ascot is your own little brothers you treating so.'

'Half-brother,' Ascot say.

From then on things just got from bad to worse. Ascot look like he vex cant done at Clemmy and the wife and the stepfather look like they vex cant done with Ascot. So finally Ascot say, 'Come let me take you all home for I have to get back to Kingston tonight.' But by this time Dagoman face set and he say he prefer to walk and Miss Clemmy and the children get into the car alone and even though Miss Clemmy look like she going to cry you can still see that she feeling proud to have her son driving her in car. But as they drive off all we can hear is Ascot a shout at the children to take their dirty foot off the car seat.

By the time Ascot get back he grinning all over again like old time but you could see that everybody feeling kind of shame and just waiting for him to go. So he finally jump up and start kiss us goodbye only when he put out his hand to Papa, Papa wouldn't take it though he shake hands with the wife and talk nice to her for he say afterward that she was a nice mannersable woman and is a shame that she mix up with a criminal like Ascot. So at long last Ascot and he wife drive off the way they did come with plenty of horn blowing and hand waving.

Mamma was the only one that wave back though and long after the car out of sight she there waving and smiling. 'That Ascot,' she say, 'fancy that. A wife with Master Degree. I did know he was goin get far you know.'

'Well he can stay far de nex time,' Papa shout out and walk out of the house.

Next day it all over the district how Miss Clemmy have daughter-in-law with Master Degree and how Ascot prosper, and hire big car and staying at hotel in Kingston. But is only me one Miss Clemmy did tell how there was not a bite to eat in the house that day and Ascot never even leave her a farthing. This vex me cant done expecially how he did gormandise up all Papa food. So right then and there I start tell her what kind of good-fe-nutten Ascot is. And is only afterward that I realise that Miss Clemmy not listening to a word I saying.

'Dat Hascot. I did always know he wudda reach far yu know,' she say almost to herself and her eyes shining like ackee seed.

# Bus Strike

## Jean D'Costa

For Roger Adams

'Get up! Get set! All hands on deck!'

A scurrying in the grass behind the low brick wall beside the bus shelter; a growl. Two empty tins rolled out of the garbage bin and came to a stop beside the lean brown dog.

'Alfonso? You lazy lubber! You have tar in your ears?'

'Me? Why you call me? Why me today? I was on the night shift!'

'Night WATCH. *Not* SHIFT. Pipe all aboard! Special duty today! Bus strike! No busses will run today. Not a single one.'

The dog put up its head and howled, waking the watchman behind the nearby plaza. The man rubbed his eyes and peered at the distant clock in the Half Way Tree clock tower. For all of his life, and maybe longer, the clock tower had stood in the middle of the four roads meeting at Half Way Tree. Sometimes its four faces told the same time as clocks set by radio stations or atomic clocks set by scientists. People called that the right time. Sometimes the Half Way Tree clock told very different times which people said were wrong.

The clock kept its mouth shut and minded its own business.

Sometimes – and this fact was known only to very very few – it could stop time altogether. But only at Half Way Tree.

A few miles away at Cross Roads and Constant Spring, south and north, time went on. Up Hope Road and down Hagley Park Road, east and west, time could keep going as usual. But now and then, a few people, just a few, would get to Half Way Tree and find they had taken no time at all to reach there. That's what they always said. 'We got here in no time at all – no time flat'.

Sometimes it stopped time in the four schools under its protection. Especially during certain nasty exams. Then the children said that they had had time to finish properly. And sometimes the clock arranged time for a sleepy taxi-driver so he could get forty winks in peace.

The watchman listened as the clock struck four. The sky had that hollow look when the dark feels the sun coming. A cool wind like lemonade ran down off the mountains behind Kingston and rolled two empty tins to the foot of the clocktower.

'Everybody here? Roll call starting and make sure you all answer up!'

'Only two trouble-makers are present, at present,' said one voice, primly.

Alfonso sighed. He wished that Cubena would learn to mind her own business. Roll call would take forever if she had to wrap her mouth around every little point.

'Silence in the ranks! All trouble-makers are doing overtime. Now stick up your ears and listen!'

Alfonso sighed again as the rollcall droned away. He answered to his name and wondered where some of the others got theirs: Spanish Flu; Gilbert Gizzado; Decimal Point; Ablative Absolute. What kind of a name was that? He was one of the oldest and crossest. Worse than Cubena. Never spoke to anyone. Talked to himself a lot, but in strange words Alfonso couldn't make out. Kept away from jokers like Tie-teet, Walk-and-Nyam, Francesca Festival and Cordelia Brown. Most people stayed away from Cordelia Brown.

The rollcall ended as the last chime of the big bell rolled over sleeping shops, dark offices, and the dusty classrooms of the schools just beyond the square.

Twenty-two miles away, Steadman Grant woke up in that same hollow dark. Every school-day he woke up the same way. He tried to shut his eyes but a light came on right behind his head. His father was up. His mother was up. His big sister Shirley was washing her face noisily. Soon they would be gone, his father to drive the van to the dairy plant out on Spanish Town Road, his mother to her day's work cleaning floors and ironing shirts for an old lawyer, and Shirley to school away in St Mary. Every working day the Grants went north, south, east, and west, or so it seemed to eight-year-old Steadman.

His father dropped Steadman off near Constant Spring, about five miles from Half Way Tree All-age school. Crowds of people swarmed all of the bus stops but Steadman paid them no attention. Half of his mind was dealing with six sevens, seven sevens, seven eights (and other versions of the six- and seven-times tables), while the other half wrestled with how to keep his lunch money away from the Grade Nine Mashers. Every day they visited Grades Three and Four for easy pickings among any small children who dared pass the school gates to buy from outside vendors. Inside, you were safe, but the Mashers knew that the best drinks and the cheapest food was out on that milling sidewalk below the clock tower, and complaining about their little ways did not help at all, at all.

So Steadman took one look at the crowds, hoisted his pack, and set off to walk the five miles. The bus-fare saved might buy him something once the rest of his lunch money had gone into the Mashers' grinning mouths.

But that day was not much like most days in school. More than half of the children never got there. Less than a quarter of the staff turned up, many of them hot, sweaty, and cross as only middle-aged people can be after walking a good few miles in the Kingston heat. Steadman took a good look at Mrs Elsie Veitch (known as 'Miss Escoveitch'): fried hair, greasy face, and vinegar mouth, just like escoveitched fish. Somebody must have taken her face when she was young and fried it dry, put it in a dish and covered it for a year with vinegar and hot peppers. And she probably soaked it overnight, just to keep the pepper and vinegar refreshed. No, he resolved, I'm NOT going to grow up like that, and turn into Mr Oldsourheavycross. Not me. Mrs Veitch lived up to her reputation: Grade Three spent the whole day doing tests, answering quizzes, and drawing plants from memory. The only comfort was that she divided her time between Steadman's class and that section of Grade Nine inhabited by the Mashers. Across the yard he could hear exclamations of,

'Boy, where is your mouth? You mean you can't spell "tangerine"? Even when you just finish eating one? And you don't know what a planet is? You don't know how to draw the flag of Jamaica? Boy, bring your book up here!'

Grade Three listened and rejoiced (more or less) in silence.

By midday the principal, a humble little man who treated all the staff and the children with great respect, announced to the assembled school that they would all leave early today.

'Please go straight home. Straight home. No loitering in the square, no stopping to buy drinks or anything else. The teachers will be on duty

211

here and in the square until all pupils have set off for home. If you can't find your way, come back here to me and Mrs Veitch.'

Of course any child would have stayed all day with Mr Wilson. No one in his or her right mind would go back to Miss Escoveitch. The school yard emptied in seconds.

Now the whole square surged with people hailing taxis, begging drives from passing cars, wiping their faces, eating patties and quarrelling with one another. In between ran the children.

A rumble from below his belt reminded Steadman that he had had nothing to eat since the hasty cup of *Milo* with sardines and bread at home. There were so many children from all of the neighbourhood schools loitering in the square that he felt quite safe.

'Move you'self, eh dog!'

The lanky brown dog stood to one edge of the sidewalk just beside Steadman. It looked apologetically at the man who shouted and reversed itself neatly around the corner by Tasty Pastry, evading the heavy feet that clumped by steadily.

'You and your dog don't know to move out of the way?' Other words, more graphic and not suitable for stories like this one, came from other hurrying men. One of them nearly knocked Steadman over as he barrelled his way to a taxi. Steadman, small for his eight years, wondered if the man had even seen him or simply mistook him for a mosquito or a fly.

As Steadman turned into the door of the shop, he came face to face with trouble: Doyle Wainwright, Masher-in-chief, capable of out-fighting and out-eating all other Mashers, stood there smiling his barracuda smile.

'Eh! Look who come to buy drinks and patty! You have money, boy?'

Silently, Steadman pulled out both his pockets for the Masher's inspection.

'Only dollar fifty? Why you so poor? Your father don't have a job?'

Very soon Steadman could see Master Wainwright placing a lengthy order up at the counter. Lots of children must be wishing that they had never come out of the schoolyard so soon. He comforted himself with the thought of the two-dollar bill hidden in his arithmetic book; Shirley had taught him how to make a secret compartment where not even the most uncivilized Kingston child would think of looking for money.

Now he hoisted his bookpack and set out to walk back to Constant Spring. Perhaps the country buses were still running. Perhaps he could buy something to eat on the way there.

He was half way across the grassy little park near the clocktower when a voice he knew rang out.

'You there boy! Grant! Steadman Grant!'

Miss Escoveitch came huffing down the road that leads from the back of the school to the square. She had two large bags in her hands.

213

'Why are you still here? Where do you live? You should be home by now!'

Steadman wished he were.

'Didn't you hear what Mr Wilson said?'

Steadman dug his toes in the ground and wished he could draw her attention to the other two hundred and seventy pupils of Half Way Tree All-age School who were sitting, standing, lounging, shrieking, yawning, laughing and otherwise passing time in the square. But no one ever pointed out the obvious to Mrs Veitch. Ever.

'Now, young man.' She heaved a heavy bag of books in front of her. 'Can you go a step with me up Eastwood Park Road? And carry these books?'

'Haven't had lunch yet, miss,' mumbled Steadman, hoping that Doyle Wainwright would get a stomach-ache from his stolen lunch and that Mrs Veitch would turn into something harmless like a garbage truck or a pavingstone.

'Lunch! No time for that if you want to get home today! Here – ' She dug around in her handbag and offered Steadman a small, tired mintball.

And that had to satisfy him as he toiled beside her up Eastwood Park Road, trying to get up the courage to tell her that he was going more or less in the wrong direction.

At the first roadblock he was glad he came with her. Angry passengers had blocked the road and were quarrelling with taxi-drivers and robot

214

minibuses making a fortune from the strike. Two trucks had stopped, unable to pass. There was no way through or around, not even for a small boy or the lean brown dog slouching along behind.

Mrs Veitch paused, looked the crowd over, and picked out a tall woman blaring out her wrath in the middle of the contestants.

'Hi there Mistress! Just a word – ' Now Mrs Veitch was up beside the woman, dragging Steadman into the middle of the crowd.

'Yes, you, lady – just a word – ' Mrs Veitch put a large arm around the woman, who seemed to wilt suddenly. A hush fell.

'Why you all stop talking? *I* am speaking privately to *this lady!*' Miss Escoveitch turned her birdpepper glare on the faces around, and the stillness deepened. 'I'm coming from Half Way Tree' – muttering bubbled up – 'in touch with Half Way Tree police station' – a new tone in the muttering – 'and both the army and the firebrigade will be moving out to Spanish Town Road. To prevent looting, fires. You know how people can go on bad. Not like you folks. And they will have to come down this very road.'

She gave them the smile that had terrified generations of children. The woman tried to pull away. The truckdrivers excused themselves and climbed back into their trucks; the minibus drivers said they would take anybody for the normal fare; the tall woman wriggled away from the heavy arm and said she could walk, God give

215

her two good feet. Everybody seemed to have urgent business somewhere else. In two minutes Steadman looked back and saw the branches and stones being heaved aside by the same people who had piled them up. The lean brown dog shied away from a stick that got thrown in his general direction.

The words of an old song popped into Steadman's mind as he looked up at the coarse red coconut matting (was it *real* hair?) which grew on Mrs Veitch's head:

'Miss Cordelia Brown, wha make your head so red?
Miss Cordelia Brown, wha make your head so red?
You tannup in de sunhot wid notting pan your head,
Miss Cordelia Brown, wha make your head so red?'

He changed the heavy bag to his right hand and walked on beside her.

Just when he could bear the heat no longer and when his arm felt as if it was stretched all the way down to the ground, Mrs Veitch turned suddenly left towards the gully that runs between Molynes Road and Eastwood Park Road.

'Hungry, eh boy? Put down the basket and let me unlock the door.'

In the deep shade of mango trees, a small verandah caged in iron grill-work opened the way into a dim, tiny house crammed with bookshelves, cane-bottomed chairs, odd tables heaped with books and papers, and a piano likewise buried under a year's collection of newspapers. Fifteen minutes later Steadman finished the last of his iced cherry drink, crackers and cheese, and accepted a thick slice of sweet potato pudding for the road. Soon he was outside, repeating to himself the instructions for finding his way by a shortcut to Constant Spring.

'Oh! It's you again!' He spoke without thinking as he turned the first corner and saw the lean brown dog ahead of him. But even a hard look could not tell him if this was the same as the apologetic dog from Half Way Tree. It was clearly very hungry, though. He could tell that. Well, he could spare some of the potato pudding. Regretfully, he pulled out the packet, took a farewell bite, and offered the rest to the dog.

It came forward carefully, sniffed, and took the slice, swallowing it in one gulp.

'Just like the Mashers. No. Not really,' thought Steadman.

The dog licked its muzzle and looked hopefully at Steadman, flattening its ears. For a while they studied one another.

'I've got to go home,' explained Steadman. 'It's far, too. Miles. And I have to get a bus at Constant Spring.'

The dog promptly retired to the shade of a hedge and lay there panting. Two empty tins rattled along the road as Steadman walked on. At the end of the street he looked back and thought he saw the dog still lying in the shade.

217

Now he had only a mile to go before reaching the terminus at Constant Spring, and, if he was lucky, he would find the country bus that he and his mother always took to get to Burnt Shop, seventeen miles away in the hills.

But at Constant Spring no such luck awaited him.

The crowds were quieter than at Half Way Tree, but much much denser. The whole of Jamaica seemed to have come to Constant Spring to catch a bus. Steadman had to squeeze and wriggle, and wriggle and squeeze to get past the market, across the little bridge, and over to the main road leading north through the hills. As for buying something to eat, that was hopeless. He began to regret meeting the brown dog.

He was still thinking about the potato pone and the raisins in it when he came to the fork in the main road to Stony Hill. On his right ran the main road where he might get a ride, if he was lucky. On the left climbed the narrow road leading more directly to Cavaliers and Burnt Shop where the Grants lived, but little traffic went that way. No one had bothered to block this road, although he had heard talk of roadblocks all over the city and beyond. He wondered if the Mashers had helped to barricade roads, and if Doyle Wainwright would actually walk home, and what his own mother would say if she knew where he was at that moment. He took a drink of water from the bottle he had filled carefully at school.

Doyle looked down on 'country people' as too stupid to live. Well, he, Steadman Grant, was a countryman and he knew how to walk far.

Ahead of him, over to the right, a dog howled. The cry sent a shiver down his back, and he turned firmly towards the old road where his grandfather, years ago, used to stride behind his donkey on the way down to Constant Spring market. The howls faded as Steadman started up the steep hill.

He had no idea what the time was. They had all been sent home at twelve, and now the sun was sending shadows across the narrow way that ran between steep banks and under the sudden shade of vast trees. It occurred to him that this road – which he saw every day from the back of the van – looked very different now that he was walking all alone.

The trees seem much taller and thicker when you stand below them and look up. In the van you rush past too rapidly to notice that enormous green lizard swinging upside down, or the way the old-man's-beard grows grey and thick on the branches. In the van you have your mother and father talking about what they have to do, and agreeing that you are old enough to go over to the tax office to collect a tax receipt after school. And they end every remark to you with 'Catch the bus. DON'T follow other children and walk home. CATCH THE BUS.' Suddenly he remembered the story of the schoolgirl who was murdered on her way home, killed down by Constant Spring gully. He began to say the nine-times table but he kept remembering more about the girl and less about arithmetic.

His nervous feeling grew as the houses along the road changed. Set far in, they offered no companionship, no sound of voices, not a glimpse of a single living soul. He was almost happy when a dumper truck piled with rocks came trundling down around a blind corner. He had to scramble up on the low stone wall to avoid being squashed flat. Then a car went by with no visible driver, just a pair of tiny hands on the steering-wheel. A pair of hands. No head, or shoulders. It went quite slowly and there was just a pair of hands, nothing else. As he tried to get a better look, the car disappeared down the road and he tripped over an empty tin rolling from the bank.

KA-POIII!

Down he went, spilling books from his bag. His bottle of precious water lay broken, and a sharp pain jabbed the hand that first hit the ground.

He began scraping up his books and wondering how he could have tripped over that tin. It was rolling away down the hill as if going somewhere in a hurry. He had the oddest feeling that it was pleased with itself. That it had set out to trip him. That it was laughing.

And now he found that his right hand wouldn't do anything but lie limp and flat at the end of his arm. The fingers tingled in a hot and cold way, and his wrist hurt if he tried to move them. His eyes burned. Painfully, slowly, he packed his bag using his left hand, kicked the broken glass out of the road, and turned to face the hills again.

Now the afternoon sun set fire to the air. There were no more trees on this five mile stretch where St Catherine and St Andrew meet. A few trucks and vans went past in both directions, those from Kingston full of people hanging on to the sides. He tried to wave to one or two but they went past as if they did not see him. The worst was being passed by Mr Stevenson's market truck. He knew it very well. Mr Stevenson lived just around the corner from the Grants, but either Mr Stevenson did not recognize Steadman, or he was in a hurry and did not want to stop.

Steadman walked on. The pain in his arm and the emptiness in his stomach took turns in tormenting him. He walked on. From time to time he heard a dog bark in the distance, sometimes behind him, sometimes ahead of him.

Now he was at last on more familiar ground. The earth changed to chalky banks at either side of the road, and down in the valleys wound narrow slanting gullies, green on their steep sides. He looked at his right hand and wondered crossly how he could ever have tripped and fallen on flat ground, he, Steadman, who could walk across the house-top as easily as across the yard, and who had climbed every tree in the Burnt Shop district.

221

Then he heard the shouting and saw the smoke ahead of him, not two miles from where the road led past his home.

He stopped.

It wasn't that he felt frightened. The odd nervous feeling had passed when he fell and hurt himself. He hadn't even noticed when it went. Now he simply knew that he should not go any further along the road. He knew it as clearly as if someone had said the words aloud. Suddenly, he thought of his mother and father, and of Shirley, and knew that they were safe from that screaming, cursing group half a mile away. In the afternoon stillness the curses came clear across the sloping hills. Horns blared out from time to time, and then would come another wave of goblin yells. He shivered and looked up and down the nearby hills.

Just below him ran a gully, twisting north and west. He rather thought it would join with the stream on Mr Hibbert's land. He climbed the low wall and jumped down, jarring his wrist sharply as he did so.

Once in the gully he found he could not see his way. The sides rose high above him, so he crawled up to try and follow it along the lip.

Balancing his bag carefully, he got between clumps of scratchy bamboo, over two walls and through no less than five fences. It was slow going, and very often he had to go aside from the right direction in order to get past some obstacle, or else he had to climb up high to make sure that he was still heading in the right direction. Sometimes the evening sun helped him, sometimes it hid in the trees altogether.

Then suddenly, very suddenly, he got over a very prickly hedge and knew where he was. Oh yes. He certainly knew where he was: he was no more than five hundred yards from home, and he was in bad trouble.

He was not in Mr Hibbert's paddock as he expected. Somehow he must have turned across the hill lower than he should have, and instead of meeting up with Joshua, Mr Hibbert's ill-tempered bull, Steadman was in the middle of the Burnt Shop balm-yard, property and premises of Bra Ramsay, also called Firecoal, Jointa, Bishop of Burnt Shop, and various other titles by friends and foes. A white flag hung from the pole in the middle of the yard where, as Doc Ramsay, the balm-yard leader healed the illnesses of his clients. Unless one was invited in on business, no one ever ventured into this sanctum, this forbidden spot.

And here was Steadman Grant, eight years old, no friend (or foe) of the man who worked miracles with bellyaches and weak blood, and who could (for a fee) give the winning numbers on sweepstake tickets to a chosen few.

Steadman turned to climb back through the hedge as silently as possible, but suddenly felt eyes on him. He froze.

223

Everything was utterly still as he looked cautiously around, the very bones in his neck creaking like old tree limbs.

The house was shut and empty-looking. The high fence hid the neighbours' houses. No one was in sight anywhere but the feeling of watchful eyes grew as he looked and looked, holding his breath.

Nothing.

He took a step towards the tall wooden gate across the yard and saw, to his dismay, the chain and padlock fastened on the inside.

He would have to climb over.

As he made to hitch his bag closer, the tail of his eye caught sight of a tall figure facing east across the valley. He thought it was a man, a man dressed in a white robe, almost invisible against the whitewashed wall of the house.

The feeling of being watched became almost unbearable.

He felt very reluctant to look properly, trying to make up his mind if he should at least say 'excuse me' or 'good evening Doc' or something harmless and stupid. He did not need to go closer to know that the figure, covered in a flowing white sheet, must be Doc Ramsay or one of his patients. NOW he was in trouble.

Then, far down in the valley, a dog barked sharply, a clear cutting bark as if to say, 'I'm running beside you, I'm here and I'm in charge!'

Creeping slowly along the fence, as far from the

figure as possible, Steadman felt rather than saw the figure standing motionless on the far side of the yard.

'You don't see me, you don't fear me,' he said loudly in his mind. Then, 'What nonsense am I talking?'

He took two slow steps. Then three. His feet wanted to run but something made them go slowly. Slowly.

The figure did not stir. The white flag on the pole in the middle of the bare yard hung limp. Steadman was almost half-way across.

Through the tail of his eye he noticed a flash of red, framed in black and white, and for the space of twelve long seconds, he turned his head and his eyes took in the frame of the figure – and its head.

The head, yes, the head had hair on BOTH SIDES. Eyes, on BOTH SIDES. The hair was white, and black. The face – no, faces – were dark red with white around the eyes. They looked both ways. They looked all ways. That was all he saw.

The figure did not move as, once more, the dog in the valley barked a drumroll of joy and defiance.

Then Steadman was beside the gate. The padlock wasn't locked after all, and he quietly began to undo it until he discovered that the wooden handle was stuck.

With a flash of real terror, he realised that

his injured hand was going to let him down. It couldn't grasp the handle, it couldn't help his other hand. It failed him.

But not his feet and legs. They could climb in his sleep. They could climb coconut trees, scaffolding, and the high brick wall by the churchyard.

Steadying himself with one hand, he dug his feet into the chainlink fencing that covered the gate, putting all of his thought to reaching the top of the gate three feet above him. Once more, the dog barked far away.

Of course he had to use both hands to swing himself over the top, and he cried out in pain as he rolled over and fell rather than jumped to safety on the other side. The dog was barking louder now. The wind snapped the flag on the pole like the crack of a whip as Steadman dropped in a clumsy heap on the ground. He lay there breathless for a while and then got himself up once more. He brushed off his clothes and picked straw out of his hair. This part of his journey would remain private as long as he could manage. He did not want to hear the lectures of his parents, the Hibberts, Miss Chen at the shop, and just about every person in the district aged forty or fifty. Even Shirley would bring it up whenever she wanted to prove that he was five years younger than her and incapable of looking after himself.

Five minutes later he was walking into the

kitchen to the exclamations of his mother and sister.

'How you got home? You feelin all right? You saw Dada? Why you didn't come with Mr Stevenson? How you got a drive? You had to walk part way? You want some lemonade? Or ginger beer? Or mint tea?'

His mouth full of ginger beer and pigs trotters with beans, Steadman answered a few questions in between his mother and sister and Mrs Hibbert telling each other what had happened to them, and how frightened they were when the fight broke out at the roadblock, and how the mob pushed a van down the hillside and set it on fire – or maybe it caught fire. And who had tried to stop the trouble, and who had a gun, and thank God nobody got shot or beaten up. They were far too excited to pay any more attention to Steadman until his mother noticed him eating his dinner with his left hand, but even the task of fussing over the sprained wrist could not stop her describing how terrified she was when Mr Stevenson's truck nearly rolled into the gully at the roadblock, and how people climbed over one another to get out.

'YOU came home in Mr Stevenson's truck?' Steadman jerked the hand she was bandaging. 'Just a while ago?'

'Your ears gone to sleep?' asked Shirley. 'I had to go down there and help her and a lot of other people. They had one big quarrel! You could hear the noise from Kingston to Montego Bay, and nobody could get past for over an hour. Some of them still down there making noise and going on bad, burning old tires like they runnin duppy.'

Far away, the dog barked once. Steadman suddenly felt very tired, the kind of tiredness that comes, he thought, after swimming all day in a heavy sea, or walking all night up the side of a mountain.

That night, very late, or very early, he came completely awake.

The night noises had all stopped. He could hear his father's breathing across the next room. His mother snored no louder than a mouse. The moonlight shone on the edge of the window, turning the frosted glass to a sheet of pearl. He felt the safe warmth of the bed, its familiar dip in the middle, the pillow tucked warm in the back of his neck. He felt floating, safe, bodiless.

He did not think of the Mashers, or of the figure in Doc Ramsay's yard, or of anything. Then he remembered that he had never had the glass of milk which, every day, he was supposed to have just before bed. He crept into the kitchen, and there it was waiting in the fridge. He watched the moonlight as he drank, and then, for no special reason, he set the half-full glass by the open jalousy window over the kitchen table, and went back to bed.

The next day was Saturday, so few people

229

minded the bus strike. In any case, buses began re-appearing by mid-morning, and by afternoon the strike was all over except for the grumblings and boastings (depending on who was talking to whom).

By Monday morning, Steadman's wrist was merely stiff and his mother had switched from telling how frightened she had been to how proud she was of an eight-year-old son who could coolly walk from Half Way Tree to Burnt Shop like any big man. Both she and Shirley forgot to ask how he got past the roadblock until the events were so muddled in their minds that they accepted his explanation of, 'Just climbing down the bank and going round.'

At school on Monday, everyone had stories too, but it was not until the following Friday that Steadman saw Doyle Wainwright in the playground, with his right arm in a cast with a queer little board sticking out for his fingers to lie on. Several children clustered around, offering to write their names and draw pictures on the cast.

Steadman stood to one side and watched.

'Broken in the line of duty,' boasted Doyle. 'Mashers know them duty and do it, and is jus bad luck why I fell down, trying to help this ole lady into the minibus. I was trying to help her an all she do is push me, y'know. Imagine a woman like that!'

Admiring noises from the fans, most of whom

230

were secretly thanking their private gods that at least one Masher was out of action for the time being.

'Wainwright! Over here!'

The crowd scattered like rice grains as Miss Escoveitch bore down on them, a bundle of papers in one hand and the other clenched into a fist. Afterwards the children swore that she hit him a knockout punch, but all she did was seize him by the collar. Behind her appeared Mr Wilson, looking mournful, and a middle-aged policeman with a notebook and hands even larger than Mrs Veitch's . . .

And time stopped.

Of course, you will say, it stopped for Doyle. Anybody – even a Masher – must know that time stops when the principal, the deputy principal, and an officer of the law invade the playground to drape up somebody. The policeman had a shabby red handbag in one hand, and Doyle, who had tried to run, stood still right beside Steadman as the three advanced on him.

In the square, the clock was striking eleven. And before it had ended its rolling, deep-toned chimes, Doyle was leaving the schoolyard with the policeman and Mrs Veitch, having recognized the handbag before being asked, and beginning a long explanation before anyone said a word.

Against his own will, Steadman walked behind them to the school gates and looked out as the little group stood for a while beside the police car.

He could not hear Doyle's voice over the sound of the bells, but his face and arms twitched and jerked as he talked and talked. The teachers and the policeman seemed to say nothing. They just looked at him. At length he got into the car with Mrs Veitch and the policeman and drove away. Only then did the clock end its chiming.

Down in the square, a dog barked. Two empty tins rolled in the midday breeze. Steadman hurried back into class and arrived early, long before the others came in from recess.

He sat at his desk and he thought and he thought, looking at his right wrist, remembering the fright on Doyle's face, the yells by the burning tires, his mother's breathless fear and Shirley's angry excitement. He remembered the two-faced mask, and how he panicked when his hand gave out at the gate. Down by the square, he could still hear that dog barking.

He gave up trying to understand any of it, and opened his history book. He liked the strange names in there: Juan de Bolas, Don Arnoldo Ysassi, Accompong.

Down at the square, after school, he saw the lean brown dog across the roadway and knew, all at once, that his name was Alfonso, and that he lived by the clock, and that he – that he – Steadman called out and ran through the traffic over to the taxi rank where the dog stood.

But he had to wait a fraction of a second to let a car pass. The clock was striking four as he raced on. The sidewalk was empty. The dog was gone.

But since then Steadman has never been afraid to walk home, or anywhere else for that matter, and he has a brown dog called 'Alfonso', although he cannot explain why he chose that name.

# Things to do – and think about

## Jean D'Costa

### Millicent

1 This story amounts to more than an amusing tale about schoolchildren. What strikes you as serious in this story?

2 There is a conflict of values in this story. How is it brought out and how is it resolved in the end?

3 What does the narrator of the story think about Millicent? How can you tell what is his or her attitude?

4 Explain the words 'Pride goeth before a fall.' Where do they come from? Do they give a hint as to what will happen in the end?

5 Do you think that Millicent would eventually become a normal, accepted member of Fourth Standard? How would this happen?

6 Would you like to belong to a class like this Fourth Standard? Why?

### The bicycle

1 What sort of athlete would Ernest Keane

make? In what other kinds of sports would you expect him to do well?

Do you believe that this story is true or not? What is the effect on you of narrative comments such as 'I know' (p. 32, paragraph 1 last line)? Who is 'I'?

3 What would you have done if you had been in Ernest's place, when his grandfather ran away?

4 What effect do statements such as 'It was only a joke. No one could have known' have on keeping the tension going in the story? This is a story-teller's device called 'foreshadowing': try to pick it out as you read.

5 How much does the teller of the story know about what is going on? How much do the characters know? How does the difference add to the spice of the story? Look up the term 'irony' and see if it fits this story.

6 Make up a story of your own starting, 'The very next day, Grampa ran away.'

## Casuarina Row

1 What sort of words does Elizabeth use? Find the unusual ones and see if you know them and if they are in your dictionary. Look up the term 'malapropism' and see if it fits Elizabeth's language (e.g. 'they didn't evaluate it', page 48, line 27).

2 How is it that the people Elizabeth invents seem so life-like and real?

235

3 Why does the writer describe Elizabeth's question, 'George, do you love me,' as 'innocent yet terrible'?

4 Why do you think Elizabeth did not come on the last Saturday?

## The Statehood sacrifice

1 What is your opinion of Latona's sacrifice? Do you agree with what she did?

2 Why is Latona unable to speak when her turn comes to describe her Statehood sacrifice in class?

3 Can we use the term 'heroic' to describe both Ernest and Latona? What sort of people do you see as 'heroic'? In what ways is Latona more than simply the main character in the story?

4 What Statehood sacrifice would you make if called upon to do so?

## Amy and I

1 What do you know that Amy's mother does not know? What is the effect of her saying that 'I feel that Amy know who the person is but she is trying to protect them?'

2 What is your opinion of the remark, 'Grown-ups are so stupid'?

3 Re-write this story as if it were a radio play. Act it out, using suitable background noises for

the ball game, the breaking window and the quarrel in the street. A tape-recorder would be helpful, if one is available.

4   What is the difference between a whole story and a single incident? Without telling an entire story as you did for Q. 6 of 'The bicycle', describe an incident in which you were helped by the loyalty of a friend.

## Peeta of the deep sea

1   Make a collection of underwater scenes which you could use to illustrate this story. Or, if you like, draw and paint a scene from this story.

2   What makes the Monster seem so terrifying? What is it and how does it work?

3   In this story, we seem to enter the world of the sea. How successful is the writer in showing us this water-world from the fishes' point of view? Can you suggest other details which could be used to expand this story?

4   Why did Peeta not tell his mother about the moonfish, even though everybody else knew about her?

5   The main part of the story is told to us from the viewpoint of Peeta and other fish. Whose point of view forms the ending, and what is the effect of 'you'? Why is the last line so tragic and so sad?

6   What strikes you as the most beautiful thing about this story?

## The Devils of Rose Hall

1 This story sounds much better told aloud than read silently. Hold a story-telling session in which you tell this and other ghost stories. (HINT: Make sure that you let out a loud scream at the point where all the ghosts vanish – it tends to frighten many of your listeners and was how my uncle always told the story.)

2 Why does the teller of this story keep mentioning 'my uncle'? What effect is the narrator trying to create in your imagination?

3 Start a collection of ghost stories set in the place where you live.

4 In what ways does the story seem real and life-like?

5 What do you find most colourful and dramatic in this story?

6 Write a story of your own starting, 'He awoke as three loud knocks fell on his bedroom door.'

7 When the challenge first comes to Rev MacGregor, the storyteller says that 'the box *was carefully emptied*'. This use of the verb is called the passive voice and it deliberately hides from us the identity of the person who emptied the box (see page 85. What are your suspicions?

## The water woman and her lover

1 Do you know any similar legends from your

own country, or from other countries? What is a 'siren' and what is a 'mermaid'?

2   Do you think that the author believes that this story is really true? Why?

3   What is your opinion of the way Big John's friends behave as the story progresses?

4   Big John is caught and enchanted by degrees. What are the stages by which he becomes bewitched?

5   Do you think that Big John's downfall was inescapable? Why?

6   Why does the water woman appear only during the moonlit nights? What effect is the moon supposed to have on human beings, as represented by such words as 'lunatic' and 'lunacy', or beliefs that you have heard of?

## Jeffie Lemmington and me

1   This is a story about a boy from the Caribbean settling down in a foreign country. Which of his new experiences do you find most striking, and why?

2   How does the boy in the story feel about his family? Can you explain why he feels like that?

3   Why are the speaker and Jeffie Lemmington such good friends? How does it help to have the story told in the first person (e.g. 'I was seven . . .')?

4 What did the two boys really feel, and what did they pretend to feel when they were running away to the country?

5 What future relationship will develop do you think, between the boys' mothers? What part of the ending gives you a clue as to how things will turn out in the long run?

## My mother

1 What particular incident or feature strikes you as the saddest and most moving in this story?

2 There are several features of the funeral that contrast sharply with each other. What are they, and how do you react to them?

3 Which of the characters in 'My mother' strike you as being heroic? How do they and their actions compare with characters from other stories (e.g. Ernest, Latona, Peeta) whom you may also see as heroic?

4 What do 'the maidenhair fern' and 'the gaudy wreath' represent in the speaker's mind? Which would you prefer, if you were in the speaker's place, and why? What emotions arise in your mind as you read the very last sentence of the story?

## The legend of Talon

1 Make a comic strip cartoon of this story.

2 In what ways does this story seem true to life,

and in what ways does it rather live up to its fantastic title, 'The legend of Talon'?

3  What do you think of the main character's attitude to himself? Can you see any echo here of the words 'Pride goeth before a fall', and a resemblance to Millicent?

4  Many of the main character's expectations form the opposite of what is really happening. This contrast is called irony: can you find some of these oppositions?

5  What do you think of the young policeman's attitude to his father?

6  How do you react to the ending? Do you approve of it or not?

## Carlton

1  This is a story about personal tragedy and public tragedy. Can you tell in what ways the tragedy is public?

2  What do you know about Caribbean history that helps you understand this story?

3  What do you think the metaphor of 'good table' signifies?

4  Find the statement that sums up the narrator's attitude to the tragedy.

5  How well does the narrator of the story know each of the main characters? How can you tell?

6  What attitude do you have to each of the three main characters? How does the narrator make sure that we take up these attitudes?

241

## Heart man

1 There are some quietly comic moments in this story. What are they?

2 What opinion do you have regarding local beliefs such as those involved in 'The Heart man'? Is Thaddeus' attitude typical?

3 How does the writer show us that Thaddeus is terrified even before he meets the old man?

4 Describe Thaddeus' changes of mood during his whole trip (there and back), and give your assessment of his character.

5 Selecting your scene carefully, draw an illustration that brings out the tense atmosphere of the story.

## The owl and the poodledog

1 Why do you think Darryll 'felt his face burn' when old Mr Benedict recognises him? What thoughts must have passed through his mind?

2 Do you think that Darryll, Joan, and Mr Benedict become friends? Why?

3 If there are wild birds and animals in your district or town, make your own museum with pictures, drawings, nests, shells, eggs, and so on, describing the different creatures and their habits.

4 If you live in the city and wild creatures no longer live there, try and find out what the countryside was like before the city grew and drove out the animals. Draw pictures of what

the land looked like years ago when it was still wild.

5  Make up an adventure story in which your pet (dog, cat, rabbit, goat, snake) is the hero.

6  Look up these words in your dictionary and talk about what they mean:
ecology    ornithology    veterinary medicine
zoology

## Anancy and Mongoose

1  If you had to give this story a different title, what would you choose and why?

2  Anancy is traditionally a trickster. What feature of Mongoose's character does he exploit in order to trick him?

3  What arguments could Mongoose have found to reject Anancy's suggestion that he move house?

4  Do you think that there is a message to this story? If so, what is it?

5  How does the language of the story tell you that it is meant to be taken as a folk tale? Why must the language be that of Jamaican Creole instead of Standard English?

## The paddy-man

1  How does the narrator's attitude to the paddy-man shift and change throughout the story?

2  What relationship exists between the paddy-man and his regular customers?

3  In what ways does this story appear realistic and true to life?

4  The theme of this story might be 'Poverty'. Describe how each character or group of characters is influenced for good or ill by poverty.

## Ascot

1  Make up a skit on *either*
   a) The ripe banana episode
      or
   b) Ascot's homecoming with his wife.

2  What do you think of Miss Clemmy's attitude at the very end when she says, 'Dat Hascot. I did always know he wudda reach far yu know,' with her 'eyes shining like ackee seed?'

3  Who is the narrator of this story? What is this person's attitude to what goes on in the story? Remember that the WRITER and the NARRATOR are not the same: the writer of a story is a real person, like you, but the narrator is pure fiction and make-belief.

4  What strikes you as the most amusing or most true-to-life incident in the story?

5  Why is this story so sad in spite of all its jokes and humour?

## Bus strike

1  What parts of this story seem real, and which ones seem like a fantasy?

2   What aspects of Steadman's character do you most admire? What details in the story support your opinion?

3   How does the author ensure that we share the narrator's contempt for Doyle?

4   Look at the language in the story, and pick out those parts which are written in Standard English, and those in Jamaican Creole. Does this pattern match how different people speak to you, and you to them, about different subjects?

5   How does the narrator of 'Bus strike' compare with the narrator of 'Ascot'? Write a character sketch of each of these imaginary persons so as to bring out how they might differ in such matters as age, background, and (perhaps) education.

# Glossary

## Velma Pollard

ACKEE  A kind of wild cashew (see *Dictionary of Jamaican English*, ed. Cassidy and LePage), called 'guinep' in Barbados, and ignored as poisonous in many Caribbean territories. Major component of the popular Jamaican dish 'ackee and salt fish'.

AFRO  Natural hair-style (replacing the processed look), which gained popularity in the late sixties and seventies in the US and the Caribbean.

ANANCY  Spider trickster hero of folk tales in many Caribbean countries; of West African origin.

BABYLON  Disparaging term used in Jamaica and originating from Rastafarian argot, describing the establishment in general; often used as specific term to denote the police.

BACKRA  A white person; also used to describe customs associated with the upper class.

BANGARANG  Jamaican creole term (echoic) for confusion.

BUSH HAVE EARS  Traditional Jamaican saying meaning there is always someone to hear what you say even when there is no one in sight.

CARITE  pronounced 'kariit'. Deep sea fish highly regarded in Trinidad.

COKEY-EYE  Cross-eyed.

CONGO  Derogatory term for black person. See *Dictionary of Jamaican English* for historical background and further details.

COU-COU  Barbadian delicacy made from cornmeal and vegetables (especially okra), turned to a smooth roundness and served with flying fish.

FLYING FISH  Small fish found in profusion in the waters around Barbados and the Windward Islands, and so called for their ability to flit above the water for brief periods (sometimes for as long as a minute).

GINNAL  Jamaican creole term for a trickster, a con-man, one who lives dishonestly by his wits.

JACKASS  Local name for donkey – popular beast of burden in Jamaica and one of the philosophers of traditional tales.

JUMBIE  Ghost, duppy.

KIN-TEET(H)  Derived from 'skin' and 'teeth' in Jamaican creole. It means buck-toothed, and sometimes a broad, insincere grin.

KOKER  Sluice gate for the canals which are very common in Guyana.

LANGILLALA  Derogatory term for a tall thin person (see *Dictionary of Jamaican English*).

MAUBY  A fermented drink made by boiling the bark of a tree, sweetening the liquor with sugar and adding spices.

MICO  Teacher Training College in Jamaica (originally for men only, now co-educational).

MILE-POST   Concrete post with mileage · computed from Spanish Town, the old capital city of Jamaica.

MUSS-MUSS   Diminutive of 'mouse'.

NECK BACK   Nape of the neck.

NIGGERGRAM   Bush telegraph; news passed from person to person ('nigger' term for a black person considered derogatory when used by whites or strangers but acceptable between friends of the same colour).

NYAM   Jamaican creole term for 'eat'.

PADDY   Rice in the husk.

PELORIE   An Indian delicacy made of split peas and spices.

PAPPY-SHOW   A ridiculous exhibition; one who makes an exhibition of himself (see *Dictionary of Jamaican English*).

RARIE-TARIE   Or 'tarry-arry'. Sweet made of sugar and water boiled to an elastic consistency.

ROLLING CALF   In Jamaican mythology, the ghost of a butcher, which takes the form of a calf often with only three legs and with eyes like balls of fire, dragging a rattling chain.

ROSE HALL   A great house dating back to the mid-eighteenth century, situated on the north coast of Jamaica, made famous by the legend of Annie Palmer, whose ghost (along with others) is said to haunt the house.

ROTI   Popular East Indian pastry served with curry.

SALITIRE   Or 'crust-cake'. Pastry made from

248

flour, molasses and spices. Difficult to swallow without a drink.

SAM ISAACS   A famous Jamaican firm of under-takers.

SAVANNAH   A common or open land used for games.

SHAME-ME-LADY MACCA *Mimosa pudica*, also called 'shame-a-macca'. A small, prickly plant with sensitive leaves that fold in on themselves when touched, presumably like a coy lady.

SOUCOUYANT   Spirit of Ole Higue in Trini-dadian mythology; a vampire, an old woman who can shed her skin, become a ball of fire and suck blood (chiefly that of children).

TALKING TO   Euphemism for courtship.

THIRD YEAR   School Leaving examination (now defunct) which served as qualification for en-tering Teacher Training institutions.

TOE-BOE   Sore toes, bruised or ulcerated.

TRUSS   From standard seventeenth-century Eng-lish 'trust': to take or grant credit for goods, especially groceries.

TULLUM   A sweet made from grated coconut and molasses.

WATER WOMAN   Also called 'Water Mamma' and 'River-maid'; the mythical lady of the river.

YA   Jamaican creole term for 'here'.

YACHTIN' SHOES   Also called rubber soles, sneak-ers, crepesoles, watchikong, plimsolls and puss boots; standard rubber-soled canvas shoes, used chiefly for sports.

# A brief note on the authors

The contributors to this anthology are all West Indian. They range from Michael Anthony, the professional author, to prize-winning contestants like Mark Alleyne, whose story was broadcast by the BBC as part of their Caribbean Magazine short story competition. All of these writers speak from the heart of the West Indian experience, even those who tell of West Indians abroad, such as Merle Hodge in 'Jeffie Lemmington and Me'. All of the writers speak first of all to a West Indian audience: most of the stories were written for local publication or with an eye to West Indian readership.

Merle Hodge, who has contributed two stories, was a lecturer in the French Department of the University of the West Indies in Jamaica, and is now back home teaching in Trinidad. A published author, Miss Hodge has brought out a novel *Crick Crack, Monkey* (1970) as well as several short stories. She almost always writes about children: a subject she knows from the inside, as well as in many different settings. On her travels in Europe and the USA, she earned her way by looking after children, and has chosen them as the centre of her professional life.

In addition to Merle Hodge, Trinidad has provided two other authors: Judy Stone and

Michael Anthony. The latter is well known for his novels and stories for young West Indians; these include *The Games Were Coming, Green Days by the River, The Year in San Fernando* and *The Chieftain's Carnival* (1993). Judy Stone works in publishing and she too was a prize-winner in the BBC's Caribbean Magazine Contest in 1977.

Our single story from St Vincent was written by a young Vincentian doctor, Ronnie Saunders, shortly before his tragic death. His colleagues at the medical school, University of the West Indies, Mona, recall him as a man of promise and sensitivity who would have had much to contribute in the field of medicine.

John Wickham of Barbados is an editor of *Bim* magazine, and author of *Discoveries* (1993). From Barbados, too, is Millis D. Nicholl, who, like Mark Alleyne, was a prize-winner in the BBC's short story competition.

Guyana is represented by David King, and, in a sense, by Ralph Prince. An Antiguan by birth, Ralph Prince has adopted Guyana as his home. He has lived and worked there for many years, and has also found time to travel throughout the West Indies. David King has done the opposite: a native Guyanese, he came to the university in Jamaica to read for the English Honours degree, and a few years later took up a post in the Department of Use of English in the same institution. His story is based on his boyhood in Georgetown, Guyana.

From Jamaica come Olive Senior and Calvin Watson, representing a literary flowering that has come about since the mid-1970s and continues until today. Calvin Watson is one of many Jamaicans who contributed to the literary section of *The Daily News Sunday Magazine*, a valuable medium for new writers in the late 1970s and early 1980s before this newspaper closed down. Much of this new Jamaican writing concerns itself with current social conditions. In the work of Olive Senior, poet and fiction writer, Jamaica of today and of yesterday are inextricably linked. Winner of the Commonwealth Prize for Fiction in 1987, Senior has published two collections of short stories, *Summer Lightning* (1987) and *Arrival of the Snake Woman* (1989), that reflect Jamaican life from the late nineteenth century until the present. Senior was editor for many years of *Jamaica Journal*, and has published widely on Jamaican history, sociology, and culture.

Like Olive Senior, Velma Pollard is one of the important talents to have gained eminence during the 1980s, a period which has seen a significant number of Jamaican women enter the literary field. Winner of the Casa de las Americas Prize (1992), Pollard has worked in as many fields as any other of these writers. Currently head of the Department of Educational Studies in the Faculty of Education at the University of the West Indies, Mona, she has published collections of her own short stories and poetry, such as *Crown Point and other Poems* (1988) and *Considering Woman* (1989), as well as studies of language usage. She is an authority on the language of the Rastafari. Married with three children, Velma Pollard has lived and worked in the USA, in Trinidad, and in Guyana, and she shares the viewpoint of the Caribbean diaspora as well as that of the Jamaican firmly rooted in her homeland.

Indeed, both editors have a great deal in common. Velma Pollard (née Brodber), and Jean D'Costa (née Creary), grew up in the country and attended primary school there in the 1940s. Later they met at the University College of the West Indies in the mid-1950s. Like Velma Pollard, Jean D'Costa has done extensive research into Jamaican Creole, in her case co-authoring two books on the historical background and development of Jamaican Creole. She taught at the University of the West Indies from 1962 to 1977, specialising in Old English and historical linguistics. Both editors also served for many years as consultants in English language and literature to the Ministry of Education in Jamaica, a commitment befitting the daughters of elementary school teachers. Jean D'Costa moved in 1980 to Hamilton College in New York State where she has added creative writing and Caribbean literature to her continuing work in Creole studies and in the historical dialectology of the English Language. D'Costa has published three children's novels (all in the *Horizons* series), and a critique of the novels of Roger Mais. Both editors are currently engaged in further fiction writing and language research.